Caffeinated

Jeannie Bruenning

To the real chick on the boat
with dry cleaning draped over her arm,
still the best hire I ever made.

Author's note:

The stories, events, and characters in this book are solely the product of the author's imagination. Any similarities between real life events and the situations in the stories are purely coincidental...but you know who you are!

PROLOGUE

If I hear my name one more time, I'm going to scream! Please, call me anything but my real name. Maybe Karen or Rachael or Phyllis... yes, that's it! I'm changing my name to Phyllis. Jenn no longer exists.

"Anyone seen Jenn?"

"No, she's disappeared."

Yes, Jenn has disappeared. I'm gone, out of sight--out of mind. I'll just sit here with my eyes closed, and they will never find me. It works for kids. But I haven't disappeared. I'm in the back room of yet one more coffee shop getting ready to open, sitting on a stool among 16 cartons of 32 ounce hot cups #573. Seriously, who decided we needed 1500, 32 ounce hot cups for a store that's never served one drink before? These are going to last us a year!

"Jenn! Where are you? The driver wants to know where to put the 20 tables and 80 chairs? Anyone seen Jenn?"

Well, I say he can stick the tables and chairs wherever he pleases. I can't face another delivery driver after this morning's insanity. Imagine pulling up to a store with almost a ton of green coffee beans and expecting us to unload the truck. Imagine 32 fifty-pound bags of coffee on a truck with no back lift, not even a hand truck! How did he think we would get it off the truck? God, how did I get into this again? I said I was finished. I had opened my last store, and promised myself I'd never do it again.

"OK, now I'm nervous, no one has seen her? Jenn?"

"Check the patio."

Whew! Yes, check the patio, maybe I'm out there enjoying a glass of wine or better yet, a Tequila Gimlet. Wouldn't that be a lovely way to open a store? Gimlets for everyone! That would be magical. Wake up idiot, you know they'll eventually find you. Unless--I can devise an escape plan. I get it... I know everyone is excited about getting the new store ready to open. Frankly, I am, too; or at least I was, but I'm exhausted. I can't answer one more question or accept one more delivery.

I have to escape. I know, I'll sneak out the back door, hop into my car, and take off! They'd see me peel off and come running out, chasing me down as I pull out of the parking lot and onto PCH 1. But I wouldn't stop. I'd keep going until I found a beach and drive straight into the ocean. I doubt even that would stop them. As the car is filling up with salty water, I'd hear them yelling, "Jenn, before you drown, where do we put the grinder?" Sometimes the responsibility of managing another café feels like a life sentence. Unfortunately, it's my life sentence. Crazier yet, I chose it. Someday, I'll be found beside a coffee roaster in some coffee shop, slumped over, having taken my final breath, my heart giving out as I pour my last scoop of green beans into the hopper.

"Hey, Jenn, there you are!"

Busted.

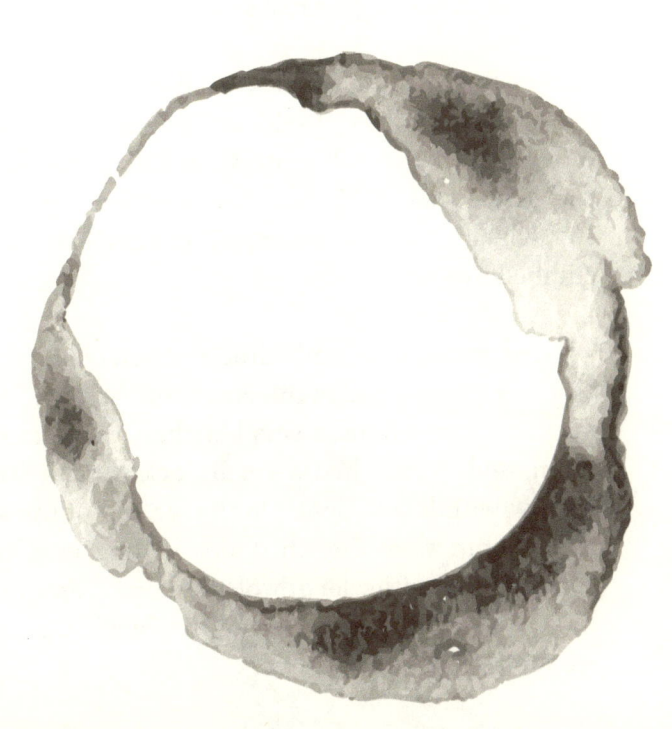

1 | The Beginning

A Messy First Impression

"How'd it go?" I heard him call from upstairs as I entered through the servant's entrance. That's what we named the door leading to the garage in the first home we owned. When the kids were little, they had actually painted a sign reading: 'Servant's Entrance' which has proudly hung on every garage door since. The kids are grown and starting lives of their own, and I'm still waiting for real servants to use their entrance.

"Interesting," I shouted back. "Tell you all about it once I get out of these clothes," I said, as I climbed the five stairs that brought me to the real front door, the door that normal people use. I removed the jacket that completed my interviewing suit, which I had adorned myself in earlier this morning, and climbed five more steps.

We had rented this two-bedroom beach condo three months ago, when we arrived in this small tourist town. It was perfect for just the two of us; a small kitchen, fireplace in the living room, and it even had a small back yard. It was long and narrow with lots of light. On the far end of the second floor living room were French doors leading to a balcony that spanned the entire length of the house. From the balcony, there was a panoramic view of the Pacific Ocean. It's where we spent all of our free time.

We had been newly transplanted to this little piece of paradise. We were big city folks who had lived in the heart of Chicago. Now, we were trying our hands at being beach bums. This new life made us feel like we were permanently on vacation, only with jobs.

I made a pit stop in the bedroom, exchanging the rarely worn navy suit and heels for my afternoon beach bum look: shorts, tank top, and sweater. Barefoot and looking as if I'd lived on the beach my entire life, I headed for my favorite spot in the world, our front balcony. The other person who also occupied this home was the man I have been married to for the last twenty-some years. As I walked onto the balcony, he greeted me with a smile and my favorite drink.

"So, tell me about it," he said, handing me my party glass. I have five such glasses. These colorful vessels perfectly hold a shot--and on some days two--of tequila, the juice of two fresh limes, a drizzle of agave sweetener – the nectar of the gods – and ice. It's my *Tequila Gimlet*, and I'm happy to have one anytime, anywhere! But, especially on the front balcony.

Plopping down in the empty chair, I reached for the glass. "Tell me if I'm wrong," I began. I can say such things with great confidence because this man that I have been married to for twenty-some years is very honest, sometimes too honest. He risks telling me the truth, even if it may hurt my feelings. This is a trait that's taken me twenty years to accept. Honesty, in spite of feelings, would not have been on my list of desired characteristics in a partner when we were first married. But, finding myself with someone for more than half my life, having raised and sent off two children, and faced with the decision to either begin to appreciate those traits you've resented for so long, live alone, or find someone new. I had recently decided to try the appreciation path; it seemed much easier than the other choices offered to me. Honesty was not a trait I felt justified ending a marriage over, even if the delivery lacked compassion.

I continued, "If you had an appointment to meet with someone in a restaurant at one in the afternoon, would you think it included having lunch together?"

He took a drink from his pint glass that I knew all too well had to be an IPA and contemplated the question. "First, having an interview in a restaurant is strange. But yes," he said, with a nod, "I would have assumed that food would have been involved. It wasn't, I take it?"

"Correct, there was no lunch involved. However, it's a cute little place; they serve breakfast and lunch. Looks like a great breakfast menu, we should go sometime." I paused and took another sip as I gazed out over the ocean hoping to see signs of whale life.

"The interview?"

"Oh yeah, when I got there, I told the hostess who I was there to meet. She told me to have a seat and I did. A few minutes later a guy came over, introduced himself, and said it would be just a few minutes and that I should make myself comfortable."

"Did I look uncomfortable?" I asked the man I call husband but his mother calls him Daniel. He shrugged.

"Another five minutes and a woman came over and introduced herself. It sounded like she said Mitchell, but it was actuallyMichelle. 'Follow me' she instructed."

"Walk this way," Daniel said in his best Young Frankenstein imitation.

"Exactly," I chuckled. "When she turned around, I hunched over and dragged my foot. The hostess saw me so I thought I better straighten up."

"I would expect nothing less," Daniel assured.

"She led me to a corner booth. We stopped and she motioned me to scoot in. I looked down at the seat, there was a fresh butt indentation. Then I looked at the table, it was piled high with dirty dishes. Apparently, there had been others sitting at this table before I arrived and had just finished lunch. There were a ton of dirty dishes. I looked around to see where the rest of her party was hiding. Surely someone else had to be joining us. There's no way she had eaten all that food."

"You're kidding, right?" he said, as he raised his glass again.

"No! After I scooted in that same guy joined us. It was just the two of them, the lady that brought me over and this guy, that's all. I cleared the spot in front of me. Either they didn't notice or didn't think anything about it. I sat at the table looking at the remains of their meal. It must have been quite a feast. My stomach had been growling but the sight of the globs of ketchup already drying on the plates made me nauseous and I lost my appetite. Good thing, 'cause they weren't intending to feed me. There was dirty silverware and empty cups with lipstick on the rim. There were a lot of dishes, did I mention that? I can't imagine all they ate. Who knows, maybe they had been there since breakfast. It's weird, I just think it's weird."

"How was the interview?" he asked with a smirk.

"Typical. The three of us talked about the coffee companies I've worked for. The guy especially liked that I have experience roasting coffee, sounds like they have two stores opening really soon. I got the feeling they hadn't hired their managers yet. Which, to be honest, is scarier than all the dirty plates left on the table."

"How soon?"

"For what?"

"The new stores, when will they open?"

"I couldn't get a straight answer, but both locations are under construction. There's actually one about fifteen minutes from us."

"That would be great!"

"A short commute! Of course, any commute would be shorter then my last one. I loved that store. I loved that team, but I can't spend three hours a day in the car anymore. Now that we are living here, I'd rather spend that time on the beach."

"So, what's next?" he asked.

"They said I would need a second interview and someone would be calling me to set that up. Maybe this one will be after someone's dinner," we both chuckled. "I'm undecided," I said. "And after today, I'm less sold on the company than before. I guess I'll see what the next interview is like--if they call." I took another sip and gazed out over the water. "It seems a little unorganized."

"Organization. That's what you do best."

"I know, but I really think I would like to walk into a place that knows what they're doing." I took another sip of my drink. "Who knows...maybe no one really knows what they are doing?"

"If this doesn't work out, there will be some other place for you."

I looked hard at my husband. "I'm not sure how I got to be the one that has to change jobs so often. Why did you get the stable career?" He took another drink, smiled, and winked.

Three hours later, my phone rang. It was the woman who ate lunch without me. She gave me the date, time, and place where I would interview next. I couldn't help but wonder if she was sitting at her kitchen table.

The Perfect Cup

The freshest beans + filtered water = the perfect Inkwell Cup

2 level tablespoons for each six ounces of water. Spread the grounds evenly in the coffee filter. Water, preferably filtered, between 195 and 205 degrees.

Only brew once, grounds should never be reused.

2 | Another Interview

Two days later, I found myself pulling the interview suit out of the closet. Armed with a resume, I made my way to a café about an hour away. As I pulled into the parking lot, a billow of smoke erupted from a metal chimney. I knew the smell; a batch of coffee had just finished roasting. The air was filled with its unmistakable aroma. As I entered the front doors, I was immediately drawn into the vibe inside. This was the real deal. It was what cafés were meant to be. Every table was filled, there was a line of customers at the counter, and no less than twenty conversations filling the space with a medley of words.

It takes a lot of effort to make a café run smoothly. I know, I've been doing it for twenty years. It's the highest level of controlled chaos you'll ever experience. I can spot a great manager the minute I step in the door. The good ones make it look easy from the other side of the counter.

I took my spot in the line of customers and recalled my first café experience. My husband's job had taken us around the country. During our journey across the states, I had worked for almost every national coffee company in existence. My first café was a wild ride. I had sent in my resume, which contained no real previous management experience, and to my surprise was called in for an interview.

The interview location was the address of a hotel. I'd had interviews in conference rooms of hotels before but this meeting took place in a bedroom suite. In fact, it was the room of the two men holding the interview, and by the look of it, they had been there for some time.

I made it through all their questions, and then they told me a little about the company. They were a bakery, deli, and café who roasted their own coffee. I was intrigued; I hadn't done any of those things. The next morning, they called and offered me the job.

"Let's meet at the hotel and you can fill out the paperwork, and we'll get you the training material," I was instructed.

Really? We're going to meet in your room again? I should have known it was going to be an interesting experience. We spent the next week interviewing for the remaining staff, learning about coffee, and checking on the build out of the store. It was a new mall and the entire project was behind schedule, including our store.

"There's no way this is going to work," I thought a few days prior to opening, staring at the scaffolding still standing in the center of the space.

The night before opening, we were wiping off an inch of dust from the counters, stocking the retail shelves, and roasting a few batches of coffee. As we were preparing to go home for a few hours of sleep before the doors opened to the new mall, I looked at my new bosses and asked, "What do we sell here?" We had been so consumed with the task of opening, we hadn't spent a moment to talk about what we actually sold, the menu, food prep, bakery items or coffee beverages.

They looked at me and then at each other. "I know there's retail, I get the coffee, but what food do we sell, and when are we going to learn how to make it?"

"We'll take care of that tomorrow," was the response.

That's how they did business for the next two years until the day I got a call that said, "We're closing up shop. There will be a U-Haul in the alley tonight at 11:00 p.m. and a crew of movers to clear the place out."

"Does the mall know we're closing?" I asked.

"No," was the response followed by a long pause.

"What do I do if they stop me?"

"They won't!"

Well, they did. Security arrived and halted the midnight escape. That was my first experience as a manager, baker, coffee roaster, and a bad escape artist.

And here I was again, interviewing for yet another coffee company. In all honesty, I was excited to be interviewing for this company. Their concept intrigued me; a café who welcomed artists, writers, and musicians to use it as their studio. How cool would that be?

As I stood in line, I watched the movement behind the counter. I knew every move they made; I had done it myself a zillion times. When I arrived at the register, I introduced myself.

"Hi, I'm Jenn. I'm meeting Gregg."

"We've been expecting you," the young man with pierced ears and jet black dreads said. "Can I get you something to drink?"

"That would be great," I replied. "What's brewing today?"

"We always have three coffees: a dark roast, which today is Sumatra; a light roast, Columbia; and of course, our House Blend, which we have every day."

"Gotta have the Sumatra," I said.

He smiled, "Going with the big guns. Great choice." He spun around and filled a ceramic mug with one of my favorite brews. "Here you are," he said, handing me the mug. "Gregg will be late. He called a few minutes ago and said he was on his way."

"Thanks," I said with a chuckle. *Par for the course. First interview came with dirty dishes, second comes late. They're batting two for two. This really isn't a good sign. If this is how they do business...,* I thought to myself.

"Find a seat and I'll send him over as soon as he gets here."

There weren't many open seats. I spotted a table for two in the far corner and made my way over. I chose the seat that allowed me full view of the café. After sitting down, I pulled out a copy of my resume. "Way too many coffee shops," I chuckled, as I scanned the list of former employers. I laid the paper down in preparation for this newest interviewer.

Settling back in my chair, I wrapped my hands around the warm mug and held it close. Sumatra filled the air, its aroma took me back to that first café. Coffee does that for me. It's

THE INKWELL CAFE | 19

like hearing a song on the radio and being transported to the moment you first heard it. Sumatra had been my crazy boss's favorite coffee. In our two years together, we had spent hours drinking Sumatra, he smoking, and me telling him about the business. I learned a lot in that first job. And, eventually, I actually learned was it was that we sold.

After twenty-five minutes of sipping Sumatra a tall man burst through the door with briefcase in hand. He walked over to the counter and greeted the baristas. He grabbed a mug and filled it with House Blend.

"Wimp," I thought out loud. You can always judge a man by his coffee choice. "Really? House Blend is the best you can do?" The same young man who had handed me my coffee pointed over in my direction. The tall man with a mug of wimpy coffee made his way to my table.

 I figured he was about my age. He wore belted jeans with creased legs. His pressed shirt was tucked in; I doubted that he ironed it himself. Maybe he did. Either way he looked compulsive. Nice shoes. Yep, he's one of those neat freaks--I should know, I live with one.

Setting his briefcase down, he leaned over and held out his hand. "Hi, I'm Gregg. Sorry I'm late." He had a great smile.

I reached up and we shook hands. I think time stopped for just a moment. In this life, we sometimes meet complete strangers who we have an immediate connection with when they walk into a room, or simply say hello, or shake our hand for the first time. It doesn't happen often, but when it does, it's magical. Gregg seemed to be one such stranger. I felt I had known him forever or perhaps in a past life.

For the next two hours, we discussed business, career paths, and coffee. It was like bumping into a friend from high school that you haven't seen since graduation. He understood about changing jobs because of transfers. His wife had job-hopped as well due to his career.

It only took a few short minutes of conversation for me to decide that if I had had a brother, it would have been someone just like Gregg. The secret thought of giving up one of my sisters for him was tempting. In addition to coming across as a really nice guy, I could tell he had a lot of experience. I thought that perhaps I could learn something from him. He got it. He understood business, especially business in the world of coffee. I thought I could work for him, and I assumed he would be one of those rare bosses that made work fun. We covered subjects that will never be found on any interview form. By the end of the interview, I felt I had a pretty good idea who this guy was. He certainly knew more about me than any other interviewer I had ever had.

Two and a half hours later, I was back in my car. As I pulled out of the parking lot, my phone rang. "Answer phone," I told the dashboard.

"Hadn't heard from you so I thought I'd call," Daniel said. "How did it go?"

"He was twenty-five minutes late," I said.

"Did he bring his lunch?"

I laughed, "No. No dirty plates this time."

"So, what do you think?"

"Wait, I think I have to turn soon. I'm not entirely sure of where I am. If I got here on time, you would think he could have. Hold on." Even though I was talking though the dashboard of the car, I had to concentrate. "Okay, I'm back. What were we saying?"

"He wasn't on time?"

"No, waited for almost a half hour."

"What do you think?" Daniel asked.

"Well, I'm not sure about the company. But," long pause. "I think I want to work for this guy. There is just something about him. I think he would be fun to work for. He may even be your long lost brother."

"What?"

"He reminds me a lot of you."

"Is that good?"

"Don't know. What are you like to work with?"

"Don't know, never worked with myself."

"Well, you're no easy ride to live with," I assured.

"You don't know how good you've got it," Daniel replied.

"Yes I do, but only because you tell me so often enough."

"How did this lost brother of mine leave it?"

"Said someone would call me within the next week. Oh wait, I have to turn again." Silence. "You still there?"

"Yes."

"Incoming call," the dashboard interrupted.

"Who's that?" I didn't recognize the number. "I've got another call, I'll call you back."

"Maybe it's him."

"Ha! It would be very surprising if they could turn around an offer that quickly."

"Call me back – love you."

"Switch calls," I said.

"Switching calls," the dashboard replied.

"Hi, this is Jenn."

There was a pause. "Oh...hi...thought it was your answering machine."

"I get that a lot. I have to figure out how to answer my phone more abruptly.."

"It's Gregg. It was great meeting you and I'm excited to be able to offer you..."

For the next few minutes I was given all the details of the job: salary, benefits, and hours. There was even a scheduled time and place to fill in the necessary paperwork for employment.

I tried to repeat every detail in my mind since I wasn't in a place to write anything down, and the voice in the dashboard wasn't willing to take notes. When Gregg finished talking, I accepted the position without hesitation. I repeated the time and place where I was to report one final time, hoping that it would stick in my head. I thanked him for his time and opportunity, and we said goodbye.

"Call Daniel's cell phone," I instructed the car.

"Calling Daniel's cell phone," the car replied.

"Hey there, it's me."

"That was fast, who was it?" Daniel asked.

"It was him, Gregg."

"Really? That *was* fast. What did he say?"

"He offered me the job."

"Seriously? What did you say?"

"I took it. Seemed silly to tell him I would think about it, after all, I'm the one that contacted them."

"When do you start?"

"Monday."

"Monday... Holy cow!"

"I know. I think they are desperate. Probably could have asked for more money, huh?"

"Oh well, you can ask for that later. Did he say what location you'll be managing?"

No, I'm guessing I won't know for a few weeks."

"So, how do you feel?"

"Still seems really unorganized, but no place is perfect. At least I know coffee, that always helps. Please tell me we will be staying here for a while? This job hunting sucks."

"I know. I'm sorry."

"Don't you want to know what they're going to pay me?"

"I'm sure it's not enough," he said.

"Nope, is it ever?"

"You can tell me at home. I'll leave here around 5:00 p.m. Meet me on the balcony?"

"It's a date. Got beer?"

"I'll pick some up."

How Long to Hold Coffee

Drink your fresh coffee right away for the best flavor.

Coffee will break down quickly if left on a heat source and coffee should never be reheated or microwaved since both of these break down the coffee flavor.

If you want to keep your coffee hot without affecting the flavor, it's best to use either an air pot or a stainless steel thermos. Both of these methods will keep your coffee hot for about an hour.

3 | Opening

Four weeks passed and I hadn't sat on my beautiful balcony once. The company I now worked for was opening two stores within weeks of each other, and they were desperate to hire managers. They had offered me and another applicant managerial positions at the same time. Because of the time crunch, the two of us burned through an in-depth six-week manager training program in half the time.

The biggest challenge of training for a store manager of a café is learning the menu; that's the "what do we sell here?" part of training. This isn't the 12 or 15 drink names that fit on the menu board, rather the 200 drink recipes that are most popular. It's estimated that there are over 80,000 drink combinations possible in the average café. Those 80,000 beverages start with three simple drinks: drip coffee, espresso, and tea. Once the menu is mastered and the time is spent on the bar making those 80,000 drinks, the rest is basic management: hiring, training, inventory, ordering, payroll, budgeting, profitability, HR, customer service, local food service requirements, company policies and procedures, core values and agenda, and everything else.

I insisted in being involved in the hiring and training of my new team. It's a manager's nightmare to be stuck with someone they didn't hire especially if they aren't any good. I'd rather stick forks in my eyes than spend eight-hour shifts with someone who isn't competent, interesting, or at the very least, funny. Being part of the interviewing and selection eliminates enormous potential issues down the road.

With most of the staff in place and majority of contruction signed off on it was now time to begin receiving all the stuff that fills a store. A large freight truck filled with 90% of everything we needed to set up our store drove into the parking lot. The truck driver pulled around to the back entrance and unloaded pallets of supplies and furnishings. There were leather chairs, floor and table lamps, pictures, framed posters and menu boards, cases of cocoa powder, caramel, vanilla syrup, and smoothie mix. Stacks of each cup size arrived accompanied by cases of lids, cup sleeves, stoppers and straws. And everything had to fit somewhere within our four walls.

My team of 20 and I had put in two and a half long days of set-up. The next day would be our Grand Opening. It had been advertised and a few thousand post cards had been sent to the neighborhoods surrounding the store. I sat in the back room on a stack of printed paper bags, surrounded by cases of cups, wondering how the hell I had gotten myself back into this situation.

I jumped as the back door flung open and Jack, a young college student I hired as a barista, came bolting through. "Jenn, the inspector is looking for you!"

"No," I responded.

"No, what?" he asked.

"No, I'm not here!" I said shaking my head.

The new barista just looked at me. "But you are. You are right there," he said pointing at me with his coffee covered index finger.

"Yes, I'm there--but I'm not here." I sat looking up at him. He stared at me for a moment and I stared back.

"He's over there," Jack finally said. "He just finished up."

After a long twelve-hour day all the inspections were complete and the final boxes unpacked. I sent the team home and began my final inspection of the store by making my way to the front door. I wanted to enter as if I were a first-time customer. I wanted to see the store through their eyes, not my tired, frustrated blurred vision. I stood looking out the front door. The parking lot was sparsely scattered with cars. I turned as if entering the store for the first time and felt overwhelmed by its size and beauty.

The store was lined with windows looking out over rolling hills that floated down toward the beach like a green magic carpet. To the left of the front door was the bakery case, a three tiered lit case where empty baskets were lined up waiting for tomorrow's fresh baked delicacies. It had a cold compartment at the bottom now filled with bottled juices and water. I straightened each row making sure the labels were centered.

 Three registers sat on the counter next to the bakery case. A description of our coffees, plus an array of goodies were neatly lined up around each. A few feet past the registers was one of the two most admired pieces of equipment in the place, our brass plated espresso machine.

This is what we referred to as "the bar." Nestled between stacks of cups on one side and an array of flavors and toppings on the other, sat a custom-made brass espresso machine, an exact duplicate of a European cappuccino machine. However, this one had the capability and speed that once was only dreamt of. This was not an automated machine, there was no button pushing, no programming. It had knobs and wands, circular temperature gauges, and an eagle perched proudly on top. If one wanted to be a barista, one needed to know about tamping, frothing, pulling shots, and adjusting the grind. There were a series of tests and certifications required for anyone who had the desire to be its operator. If you didn't pass the grade, you didn't work the bar. You couldn't fake your way through this one, if you didn't know what you were doing, it was obvious.

Just beyond the espresso machine was the door leading to the back room, which was a world of its own.

The right front corner of the store was home to the second most admired piece of equipment, a large blue and silver Probat Coffee Roaster. It looked like a miniature train engine waiting at the station. When the coffee was roasting, rich earthy smoke came out of its chimney. Around it sat burlap bags filled with green coffee from far off ports such as Costa Rica, Sumatra, Java, and beyond.

Four large glass garage-style doors lined the wall beyond the roaster. When weather permitted, which was most of the time here on the West Coast, these doors would roll up, opening the café to a huge patio. In the back corner was an oversized fireplace that could be enjoyed by those seated in the café and outside on the patio. Finally, sitting across from the fireplace was the bakery, where all the day's delicacies were created. This was the largest café I had ever seen, and it was mine.

The sign above the door read, Inkwell Café, a creative café. There was nothing we served that was not created on site. We roasted our beans and baked our croissants; we shaved huge chocolate bars to top our mochas. What set the Inkwell Cafés apart, and what had intrigued me the most, was that we welcomed writers, artists, all creative types to spend the day with us--creating. And they did, from early morning 'till closing.

 The view from the patio was breathtaking. Along the rails of the patio were easels to hold canvases. There would be daily painting classes held on the patio and live music, typically from singer songwriters that needed to test their newest creations. During the week, guitar lessons would be scheduled in front of the fireplace. Authors could have book signings in the store and photographers could sell their masterpieces. If you couldn't find your muse at the Inkwell Café, she wasn't to be found. The energy alone kept you inspired and at times unable to catch your breath due to the enormous rush of creativity that propelled its way through the café.

That is how it was supposed to be. That was the unproven vision for this location. With my checklist complete, it was a few short hours away from the Grand Opening, which would be our trial run. There had been three long days assembling tables and putting them in place. We set up the area around the espresso machine, merchandised the shelves and stocked the back room.

We spent this last day making sure everything was prepared for our first guests, mopping the floors and wiping off the newest layer of dust that had settled from all the unboxing. The staff was as prepared as a new team could possibly be. Our three coffees had been selected and written creatively on the Coffee Board with multicolored paint pens; there had been a final check of the restrooms for toilet paper, hand towels, and soap; and the boxes of free mugs and t-shirts we'd be giving away the next day were stacked against the side wall.

It was picture perfect. Everything was new and clean and fresh. It had that new store smell. The smell of leather, wood, and coffee filled the air. I stood there with a smile on my face and my eyes closed breathing it all in, and for a moment, all the tiredness left me. I stood in the quiet bliss when I was interrupted by a tapping on the door.

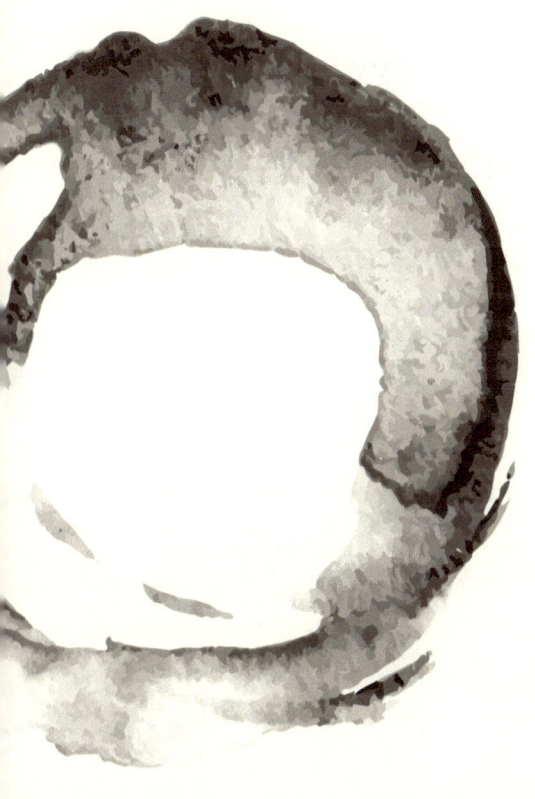

NOW HIRING

Full and part-time
positions available.

Apply on line:
create@theinkwellcafe.com

Walk-in interviews
9:00 a.m. - 3:00 p.m.
Monday - Friday.

Bring resume, energy,
personality, and a smile.

Inkwell Cafe

4 | The Chick On The Boat

Tap, tap, tap.

"We open tomorrow," I said, sticking my head out the door.

"Are you hiring?" a woman asked.

We've hired, I thought. *We've been hiring for three weeks, where have you been?*

"Yes, we are," I said, silencing the sarcastic bitch in my head and acting as professional as possible. "What are you looking for?"

"I'm available full-time," she said with great confidence.

I don't know why I did it, but I pushed the door open and said, "Come on in."

The mystery woman, who appeared to be in her early thirties, walked through the front door. It was only a guess but I'm usually pretty good at figuring out ages. She had dry cleaning draped over her arm and she looked a bit wind-blown. I locked the door behind us, and then turned around.

I watched as she walked into the middle of my beautiful store and peered out as if she was looking at the Grand Canyon for the first time. I then noticed something. There was a visible energy running through the empty café. Heat waves seemed to radiate from the woman beside me and consumed the vacant spaces in the room. It was as if the tables and chairs were breathing and the planets had aligned. Had I looked up I might have seen stars suspended from the ceiling. It was like we were in a movie where an unexpected wind blows through the window, causing the curtains to flutter and things to fall off the counters. I felt her energy.

"It's beautiful in here," she said.

"Thanks. I think so. New stores should look beautiful." I stood behind her, watching. She scanned the café.

"Roaster?" she said pointing to the Probat.

"Yes," I nodded.

"Never seen one up close," she said. "Love the leather chairs."

"Me, too."

She walked a bit further and pointed outside. The sun was setting and the sky was a watercolor of orange, yellow, and pink. "That's a big patio."

"I know," I said. "I love it. We can seat almost as many people out there as in here."

"And our view," she said.

Our view? I thought. *Our view? Hold on sister. You don't have a job yet, you're interesting, but...!*

"Yes, the view is amazing. Someone was thinking when they got this location," the manager me said.

She turned around and glanced down at her dry cleaning, "I don't have a resume. Sorry, I didn't think I would be stopping for a job." She laughed, lifted her arm slightly showing off the dry cleaning and brushed her bangs back.

"That's ok," I said. I couldn't see her newly cleaned garments clearly because of the large white logo that spanned the length of the plastic bag. Didn't look like anything too unusual. No clown suit or evening gowns. "Have you worked in coffee before?"

"No," she replied with a look of innocence.

No coffee experience registered in my head. "And you would like full-time hours?"

"Yes. I have open availability. I prefer mornings, but I can work anytime."

"That's a plus. When would you be available to start?"

"Well, that's the thing." (There is always "a thing".) "You see, I'm leaving tomorrow for a two week vacation."

"Are you working now?" I assumed.

"No," she said wide-eyed and smiling.

Vacation from what? I thought. I must have given her the look of please continue--because she did.

"I do this thing every year with my friends. We'll be on a boat for two weeks."

"Oh, a cruise."

"No, not really," she said waving her hand in front of her as if to say, you silly girl. "It's their yacht."

"Yacht? That's awesome."

"But as soon as I get back, I'm all yours."

Now she was very interesting! I reached over the counter and grabbed a business card. "Here's my card. Give me a call when you return."

She held out her hand, "Thanks. I'm Suzie, by the way."

I held out my hand, realizing that we had not done our introductions, "I'm Jenn."

She looked down at her watch, "Oh, I've got to go, five more stops before I get home. I'm really not ready for this trip."

"Well, thanks for stopping by. It was," I paused. "It was good to meet you."

"Crazy! I know! It's just crazy! Stopping to inquire about a job..." she raised her arms again displaying the dry cleaning. "Thanks again, I'll call you as soon as I'm back. I'm excited. It's going to be a great place to work!"

I immediately began to play back our conversation in my head-- *I didn't offer her a job, did I? I didn't make any promises... she's just getting ahead of herself, isn't she?*

"Call me when you're back in the area." I opened the door for her.

"Have a great Grand Opening! Wish I could be here for it," she said.

"Have a great trip. We'll talk when you get back."

"Bye."

I locked the door and stood watching as she half ran to her car. I was curious as to what she drove; a small sports car perhaps, or maybe a carriage with six white horses, she was that kind of person. I was a little disappointed as she unlocked the doors of a green four-door Prius. She carefully placed the dry cleaning on the hook above the back door, and as she closed the door, the wind caught her scarf and it flew up behind her. She grabbed it, dropped herself into the front seat, closed the door, and she was gone.

"Crazy?" I said to the emptiness. "It's all crazy. It's a crazy company that thinks you can hire a manager and open a new store in less than a month. And now--crazy strangers who assume they will be my next employees." I walked back to the counter. "Shit, I didn't get her information."

I put the large ring of keys in the pocket of my black apron and thanked God our aprons were black and not some funky color that wouldn't hide the coffee and cocoa, which was sure to accumulate throughout a normal day. I then headed toward the back room for one final walk through.

"Doesn't really matter, I guess. I may never see her again." I swung open the door to the back room and it slammed against the wall. "Really? No one thought to put in a door stop?" I walked to the back and stood in front of the large electrical panel and began flipping the store lights off.

I heard a deafening CLICK echo through the back room. It sent chills to my spine. I nervouly scanned the room. "What the hell?" I held my chest trying to prevent my heart from bursting through. I looked at the back door waiting to see the person who made such a noise. With a sigh of relief, I didn't see anyone. I slowly crept to the door. As I passed the magnetic strip that held an array of kitchen knives, I grabbed the biggest one. Finally, at the door leading to the dining area, I peered through the small window. I couldn't see any bodies.

I slowly pushed open the door and yelled back in the deepest and broadest voice possible, "Jack, I'm just checking the front door. Hang tight, I'll be right back." I knew there wasn't any Jack waiting in the back room, but the presumed intruder didn't know that. I looked out into the front of the store, "I think I'm alone, at least I hope I'm alone. It's way too early in this career to have headlines that read, *Store Manager Found Ground in Coffee Grinder..."*

Scanning every darkened nook and cranny I saw no one. Feeling a bit calmer, I returned to the back room. A loud hum was coming from the fuse box. I made my way over to it. I flipped the silver latch and opened the door with one hand while holding tightly to the twelve-inch knife in the other. Twenty some switches sat proudly in the "on" position. Above this box was a small electrical box with the word SIGN written across it in black permanent marker, followed by "Do Not Open." I put my hand on it, it was purring like a large lazy cat. "It's the sign light, it has to be," I said in an attempt to calm my nerves, still trying to talk myself into the idea that there was no serial killer in the store who used coffee grinders as a means of disposing of his victims.

Convinced the case of the loud click was solved, I walked over to the desk and scanned the next day's schedule. "She's going to be on a yacht for two weeks? What do you do on a yacht--for two weeks? And she wants a job serving coffee? I don't get it." I returned the knife and grabbed my bag and coat and headed to the front door and took one final look of the café. It was beautiful, most likely the most beautiful café I had managed.

The past four weeks had been a flash. New job, new store, new staff--it was crazy. I let myself out, locked the door, and made my way to my chariot, otherwise known as a VW Jetta. I unlocked the door and dropped myself in. As I placed the key in the ignition, I was overcome with a crazier feeling. For the second time in a month, a complete stranger had walked into my life, and I felt an instant connection. I had already decided that I would hold a position open for the chick on the boat. I also knew she would be most likely the best hire I would ever make.

GRAND OPENING!

Doors Open at
8:00 a.m.

Free T-shirts to the first
500 customers!

Free Inkwell Mugs
while supplies last!

Live Music

Inkwell Cafe

5 | The Grandest of Grand Openings

I arrived home too late to watch the sunset and too tired to do anything but take a shower. One of the side effects of working with coffee is that the smell comes home with you. It only takes a few days of employment before your car, closet, clothes, shoes, hair, skin, and even pillow absorb its aroma. It's almost impossible to come home from a day spent with coffee beans and not want to throw yourself into the shower. I crawled into bed and got through perhaps the first two minutes of "As Time Goes By," my favorite BBC sitcom, and I was out.

The alarm sounded at 5:00 a.m.--coffee is an early riser. The Grand Opening was advertised for 8:00 a.m., typically a late start for a café. After today, we would welcome our guests at 5:30 a.m. every morning. I showered again and dressed. I got in the car and headed back to my new second home. I turned into the parking lot at 6:00 a.m. "Holy Crap!" I blurted out. To my surprise and horror, there were twenty people camped out in front of the store. I parked and waited a few moments. "This is nuts... We're not open for two hours..." Two more cars pulled in to the lot and six more people lengthened the line. "My team has never worked together... this is our first day..." For the first time since the beginning of planning for this Grand Opening, I found myself relieved that Gregg had arranged backup for us. Three other managers were scheduled to fill in short shifts. Each was bringing one or two seasoned staff to strengthen our workforce. My only hope was that they knew what they were doing.

I forced myself to get out of the car as three more cars pulled in. "Good morning," I said as I approached the door. "What time did you all get here?"

"We were here at 4:00 a.m." The first customer in line said quite proudly.

"We're excited you're opening," said another.

"Obviously," I said.

"We're ready for our free t-shirts and mugs!"

I unlocked the door, acknowledged them again with a nod, and quickly locked the door behind me. There was a reason I was there two hours early, and as much as I wanted to offer them a cup of coffee, I wasn't there this early to serve our waiting customers. They would have to wait a bit longer. I turned, and once again took in the beauty of this new, clean, and untested store. Today would be the maiden voyage. Today everything would be tested and by the growing line outside the doors, I knew it was sink or swim. We were going to be baptized by fire, and the flames were already being fanned.

I walked into the back room and approached the dreaded fuse box. I placed my hand over the box labeled SIGN, it was still humming. I opened the forbidden box and found a large dial that roughly resembled a clock. A silver hand pointed to 7:00 a.m., its scheduled turn off time. I closed the box, ensuring the latch clicked and swung open the large panel beneath it. I flipped on every switch, and the building came alive. I set down my bags and walked back out into the café. I could see the line of eager coffee drinkers had now turned around the corner, and figures were lined up along the far side of the building.

I switched on the espresso machine and placed my hands on its side waiting for the boiler to kick on. "You can't let us down today; by the looks of it, we're going to need you in full force." I patted her side and she began to hum. I filled the small silver basket with espresso and carefully placed it in its proper place on the machine. Grabbing the large black knob, I began letting the water flow through. Dark, rich, espresso filled my small cup creating a delicate layer of crème on the top. "Perfect," I said as I brought it to my lips. The greatest perk of this job is starting each morning with a small cup of perfection. I slowly sipped the tonic as I watched a few more cars, and just as many customers, pull into the parking lot.

Seven a.m. arrived as did the first wave of staff. The line was now winding around the building.

"How long have they been here?" My eager new employees asked.

"I got here at 6:00 a.m. and it was already forming."

The morning preparation for getting a café open is perhaps the busiest time of the day. Coffee needs to be brewed, then we pull fresh croissants, muffins, and cinnamon rolls out of the oven and arrange them perfectly in the case. The espresso machine takes time to get fired up and a few test shots pulled. Then, there's double checking to ensure the mocha, ice tea, and iced coffee are in plentiful supply, the ice bins filled, the restrooms checked, and money counted. This morning there were a dozen or so boxes of free t-shirts and mugs that were stacked against the wall. Our scheduled musicians arrived and were setting up next to the fireplace. Creamers were filled, sugars stocked, and money put into the registers.

This new team that I had assembled stood around the espresso machine for a few last minute instructions. Our barista had set out eight 2 oz. cups containing a spoonful of white chocolate powder lining the bottom of each. As we gathered, he began pulling shots, one espresso shot per cup. A quick swirl combined the two ingredients, and he handed it off to each team member. As we each stood gazing down into this little cup of power, our duties for the day ran through our heads.

"Guys, they've been waiting a long time. We've got to open those doors," I said. I raised my little paper cup, "Here's to the greatest Grand Opening ever!" We all gulped our little cup of splendor, an opening tradition that would remain with us forever.

"Everyone to their stations! Remember – do it right – do it well – and PLEASE - let's have fun doing it!!!" My new team cheered as if it were a battle cry. I walked to the door, took one more look back at my new, untouched, perfect store, and turned the latch.

The first two hours went beautifully. I welcomed customers at the door and introduced myself. We served samples of coffee and bakery items. We served coffee by the cup and sold it by the pound. The espresso machine was humming; it was a non-stop production of espresso, lattes, and mochas. We managed the line well, keeping customers at the register a few moments longer than usual. This wasn't difficult as introductions were being made and descriptions of our coffees offered. No sense rushing people through a line just to make them stand at the bar longer, you can only produce so many espresso shots a minute, and we were maxing it out.

Hour three came and went--a few more workers, a lot more customers. At some point, I remembered Suzie's parting words, "I wish I could be there." I was wishing that she and six more could be here. *Two weeks on a yacht?* I thought. *I hope you're worth waiting for...*

Hour four came, we were keeping up. We were tired, but we were a success, and we knew it. Calls were coming in from the home office, first to check on how things were going and then with congratulations and words of encouragement to keep it up.

Fifteen minutes later, I realized that something wasn't right. My heart stopped as I watched a young man who was standing at the end of the line of customers waiting for their drinks, walk up and take the next drink that was called.

He can't do that! I screamed in my head.

"Soy Latte with whip cream," the barista called out. The woman who had just found the end of the line began to walk forward passing the twenty customers whose faces were quickly becoming less than patient.

I walked over to the front of the line. "What drink are you waiting for?" I asked the first person in line, who was now looking at his watch. As he repeated his drink, I glanced over to the computer screen; it wasn't there. "And you," I pointed to the man next in line forcing myself to keep smiling, "What are you waiting for?" Again, I scanned the screen, praying I'd find his drink.

A team member emerged from the back room. I grabbed her and handed her a pen and paper. "We've lost these orders, go down the line and ask them what they ordered." She looked at me in horror. "Really, we've lost about twenty orders. Just go down the line and ask what they had. We'll get them made right away." She took the paper and pen and started with the first customer.

I stepped into the back room and to my great surprise found Gregg washing dishes. "Is this what you do during Grand Openings?" I asked.

"Someone has to do it," he said. "And you don't want me on your bar or near your registers."

"We have a problem." His expression changed. "The computer isn't keeping up, we're losing orders."

"That's never happened," he said.

"Well it just did. We're going faster than the system can handle. There's about twenty people waiting for drinks, and the computer has no record of what they ordered."

"Did you..."

"Yes." I interrupted. "I have someone writing down their orders now. Got any idea what we do for them for this mess up?"

"Free t-shirt?" he asked, raising one eyebrow.

"We're already doing that. Do we have any free coupons we could give out?"

Gregg wiped his hands and grabbed his briefcase. He handed me a pile of free drink cards to pass out. "Glad to know we have these."

"We don't," he said with a smirk. "These don't exsist and when they do, they are mine."

"You mean they are super secret?" I whispered

"Yes, and let's keep it that way."

"Then I'm glad you were here today." I said taking the cards. "And by the way, you may be the most expensive dishwasher I've ever had." Looking over the dishes he had just finished, I nodded, "there's a few spots on the mugs, you may have to do them again."

"You are a bitch," he said.

"You have no idea," I replied.

He laughed, and I was relieved. We hadn't worked together long enough for me to be sure he had a sense of humor, and today was not the day to find out he didn't.

I walked out of the back room with Gregg behind me. He grabbed a clean towel and headed out into the café. I made my way down the line of patient customers apologizing for the oversight and for the extra time they had spent waiting. I invited each of them to come back and give us a chance to do it right.

As I got to the end of the line, I heard the most godawful sound. It equaled third graders on their first day of band practice. I scanned the café to find its origin. Standing proudly in front of the fireplace was a middle-aged woman dressed as Mother Earth attempting to play a recorder. The string musicians sat around her with expressions of excruciating pain.

Stephanie, the woman responsible for lining up our live music, passed by, and I reach out and grabbed her arm. She flinched, as I apparently was holding on tightly as I drew her close. "I know it's our first day, and we haven't had a chance to know our musicians personally, but let's never invite her back."

"She's not supposed to be playing," Stephanie said.

"What do you mean? She just got up there?"

"I'm not sure. I'm guessing from the expression of the trio that they didn't know she was this bad."

"I've heard recorders played well, this isn't anything like a recorder being played well," I said.

"I'll talk to them. I'll let them know that this isn't an open mic," she assured me.

"If it goes on much longer, I may lock myself in the bathroom."

"I'll join you!" Stephanie said, as she locked eyes with a member of the trio and gave her the cut sign. The cellist nodded, then placed her bow on the strings, her two counterparts followed and within two measures, the recorder stopped, looked very puzzled and sat down.

"I'll talk to them at the end of their set," she said, peeling my fingers off her arm.

I quickly made my way to the bar to assist in the recovery process. For the next ten minutes, we were pushing out drinks as quickly as humanly possible. Our new espresso machine was wheezing and coughing the entire time. Gregg finished his round of the café, and as he headed towards the back room, glanced over at me.

"Good work for your first day," I said giving him the thumbs up. He gave me an expression that, if not for a café full of customers, would have been followed with a different finger up.

"Can you help us get these drinks out? They all have names written on them, just call out the customer's name."

"Sure," he said, "At your service."

Gregg played his part perfectly. He called each drink and handed them to the patiently waiting customers. Each received a personal apology along with an invitation back to allow us to do it right. Every so often he added, "It's my first day."

There was a united sigh when we realized that we were once again on track. We had successfully made the drinks for the current orders as well as the ones we had lost. In all my years at this job, I had never seen that amount of drinks created in such a short time.

We had pushed our new espresso machine to the limits. I kept finding myself reaching up and patting its sides, "You're doing great," I said. "Keep going girl, don't break on us now. You can rest tonight."

"We need to name her," I told my co-barista. "She's earned that today."

"Bertha, seems appropriate," he said.

"It does, doesn't it?" I said. "Bertha, I like it--sounds sturdy, sounds capable." Bertha made it through the afternoon and won a place of honor in our store.

By 5:00 p.m., things finally started to slow. We were out of t-shirts and only had a half of a case of mugs left, estimating that just shy of eight hundred people had been in our store - eight hundred customers on a day that was intended to be advertising, not selling. There was no longer a line out the door. There was a slow steady stream of customers coming in to check us out. Every table was full, inside and out. Conversation and laughter filled the air, and a string trio serenaded us from the back corner. Cookies, mini apple pies, and gooey brownies were being pulled from the oven.

In the back room tallies were being made. It was too early to call, but it appeared we had just had the biggest Grand Opening in the history of the company. I stood behind Katie, a high schooler who was working her first job. On her first official day in our store, she had been at the register for six hours serving an endless line of customers. All of us complained that our cheeks hurt from too much smiling. Most of our feet were numb and backs ached.

As I began brewing new batches of coffee, a gentleman walked in. Katie welcomed him, introduced herself, explained our menu board and asked what she could get for him.

"I'll just take a large coffee with half and half," he said.

Katie didn't move. It was like watching a movie freeze frame. I stepped closer. She looked down at the register and then back up at him. "Half and half what?" she said in her sweet innocent voice.

"Half and half," he repeated. She shook her head.

"You want it half and half what?" She asked again attempting to clarify her question. I was now standing next to her.

"Just a large coffee, half and half," he repeated, as if it should now make more sense.

She smiled, looked down at the register and back at him. "Half and half....," she began yet again.

I put my hand on her shoulder. "He would like a large cup of coffee with some half and half in it." I said.

"Oh," she replied. "That half and half."

I began to laugh. "I'm sorry," I said addressing the very confused customer. "It's been a really, really long day, and we're all just a little off our game."

Half and half, we were all a little half and half. We were exhausted, we were successful, and now we were all just a little bit crazy.

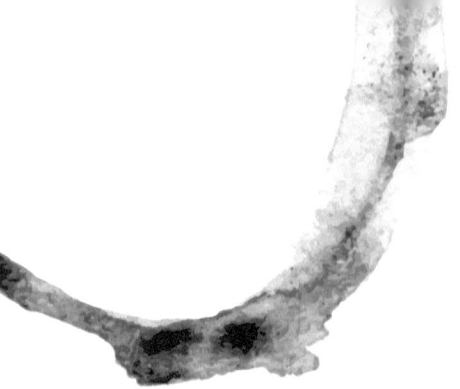

Green Coffee Beans

Coffee berries and their seeds undergo multi-step processing before they become roasted coffee.

First, coffee berries are generally picked by hand. The flesh of the berry is removed, usually by machine, and the seeds are fermented to remove the slimy layer of mucilage still present on the bean.

When the fermentation is finished, the beans are washed with large quantities of fresh water to remove the fermentation residue.

Finally, the seeds are dried and sorted. The seeds are then labeled green coffee beans.

6 | The Roaster, the Baker, and the Magic Maker

The next morning it was still dark when I was greeted by four team members at the front door at 5:00 a.m. "We survived," I said.

"Where's our line this morning?"

"Please," I said holding my finger to my lips, "don't tell anyone, but I'm so glad there isn't one!" My co-workers agreed. "Today should be normal or as close to normal as possible."

"How did we end up yesterday?" my baker asked.

"Great, I think!" I said. "We won't know 'till we pull reports today, but as of last night, it was being called a great success."

"Good," Barry the baker said. "It sure felt good!"

"It did, didn't it! Don't think I would like to do that every day, but yesterday is one for the record book," I said as we headed into the back room to turn on the lights and start our day.

There were three very essential positions on my staff. I called them the Roaster, the Baker, and the Magic Maker. The Roaster was our Roast Master, her one and only job was ensuring our coffee was the best it could be. All day long she executed taste tests of the brewed coffee as well as the espresso. This kept her on a caffeine high. She checked the dates on the coffee ensuring that we always had the freshest coffee on our shelves and scheduled our coffee of the day according to those coffees that needed to be used up quickly.

Daily she fired up the roaster and began roasting. Coffee roasting is a science and an art. Knowing what coffees blend well, understanding their unique profiles, and roasting to obtain the expected flavor takes time to develop.

Coffee is roasted at very high temperatures, and there is a very fine line between dark roast, burnt, and flames. In fact, these three results can be seconds apart. Once a batch of coffee has reached its desired roast, it has to be cooled quickly. This is done by opening the hamper door on the roaster, allowing for all the rich dark coffee beans to pour out into a large round cooling bin. At the same time, a cloud of deliciousness billows out the top of the roaster, filling the outside air with its unmistakable aroma. A four-arm rotator begins to churn the beans, ensuring that the cooling process begins immediately and is completed quickly.

Because the roasting process can be so volatile, and those amazing little beans can go from dark roast to flames so quickly, the 5 Alarm Latte was created. When coffee is over roasted, it creates additional heat and smoke that escapes inside the store, instead of being vented out where it ought to go. This action causes a reaction – the fire alarm goes off. At the Inkwell Café, the alarm is designed to be silent for sixty seconds before it sounds in full force and chases all the customers out. In those sixty seconds, it is expected that all doors can be opened to allow this uninvited heat to escape. It was also designed to give a sufficient amount of time to call the fire department and let them know there wasn't really a fire, just a lot of hot beans.

A large blue light begins to flash on the wall behind the roaster when the silent alarm goes off. Once seen, the Roast Master shouts "5 Alarm Latte," and the staff takes action. As the Roast Master tends to the roaster, one of the team members from the register catapults over the counter and props the front doors open. The second register person bolts to the back room door, props it open, then proceeds to the back exit door and holds it open. If not already open, the baker opens the doors leading to the patio. The manager, that would be me, calls the fire department. And finally, the barista begins making lattes, enough for any and all of the first responders. Since it is unlikely that the call to the fire department gets there before the trucks are deployed, we feel the need to provide our firefighting heroes with a little "thank you" for their time and efficaciousness.

Five lattes are made for the practice runs because until it happens, there's no way of knowing just how many first responders will show up. I had considered calling ahead to ask who I could expect to respond, but each time I played the conversation in my head, I realized that unless there truly was a fire, it would sound suspicious. Who calls the fire department to ask, "In case of a fire, how many first responders show up?" It just didn't play right in my head.

Our baker is the next in the chain of command. He ensures that our bakery case is filled with the most tempting deliciousness possible. He bakes large batches of product at least twice during the day. In the morning, our customers will find muffins, croissants, decadent cinnamon rolls, and cookies.

And in the afternoon, the evening fare is baked: brownies, mini pies, lemon bread, and mini apple pies. Before the night is over, a proofer is filled with the next morning's product.

The proofer is my third favorite piece of equipment in the café. It starts out as a refrigerator that is filled each night with bakery items waiting to rise. In the early hours of the morning, before anyone arrives to work, it stops cooling and begins slowly warming the product that has been put in its care. Moisture is added, which calls the yeast to action, and these delicacies begin to change shape as they rise to perfection.

When the Baker arrives, the items are ready to be placed in the oven. Within minutes, the smell of baking delicacies fills the air and dances with the freshly brewed coffee aroma. It's a dance that forces you to stop and partake. It's a dance that keeps you coming back; a dance that once introduced to your morning routine, calls you back every day. It's a dance that brings you back in the afternoon curious as to what new rhythms you may experience.

The third person to round out my management team is the Magic Maker. As the sign reads, The Inkwell Café is a creative café. It is the Magic Maker who invites the creativity to partake. It is her task to connect with the artists in the community and offer them our patio or café for lessons, classes, and shows. On any given Tuesday afternoon, the twenty easels lining the patio should be filled with canvases being painted by twenty hopeful artists. It's normal to find a small group of guitar players sitting around the fireplace learning chord structures. From open to close, at least one of the guests is writing a novel, creating a murder mystery, or editing a manuscript. It's the Magic Maker's job to make it known that the Inkwell Café is where all this creating should be done.

The Roaster, the Baker, and the Magic Maker, three vital positions, three strong individuals all needed to work together as a team. My Roaster, Baker, and Magic Maker were handpicked, and I knew I was lucky to have each one of them.

At 5:30 a.m. on our first real day of business, we once again had customers at the door. It was a good sign. It meant that the day prior was not a fluke, that we had all the makings of being a great store.

During the next two weeks there were some hiccups. One morning, the proofer's timer was not set properly and none of the morning product had risen. On another morning, the milk delivery did not come so I found myself at the local grocery store filling my car with 40 gallons of milk to get us through the morning. On the second Friday we were open, the proofer's timer once again was incorrect, and we had cinnamon rolls the size of Texas.

But with all the catastrophes, the team showed their calm under pressure and ability to have fun, no matter what the dilemma. We learned more about each other and became more confident in the roles we held. We did our best to make it look easy.

Twelve days after we opened, I realized that I was on my twenty-first day of work without a break, without a sunset, without seeing my front balcony.

I couldn't help but wonder if I would hear from the chick with the dry cleaning, who supposedly had friends with a yacht. We were growing faster than expected, and I needed to add staff. Why was I waiting for her? I hadn't even spent five minutes with the woman. But the waiting was coming to an end. If she was serious, I should hear from her in the next day or so.

On day thirteen, I left the store in time to make it home for a sunset. To my delight, there was an orange and white party glass waiting on the counter, right next to a fresh bouquet of flowers... twenty-some years has its privileges.

The Bean

There are two kinds of coffee beans, Arabica and Robusta. They have different tastes and different caffeine content.

Arabica beans are considered a higher quality bean. It is grown at altitudes over 3,000 feet. The higher the elevation the higher the quality; some are grown as high as 7,000 feet. 70% of coffee consumed is Arabica.

Robusta beans grow at lower elevations, providing different climate. Although most people prefer the taste of Arabica, Robusta has its fans.

Robusta beans have twice as much caffeine as Arabica!

7 | The People of the Well

"How's the hiring going?" The now very familiar voice of my boss asked on the other end of the phone.

"Good," I replied. "I've a good application flow, and I'm talking to a few people."

"Has the chick on the boat called?"

"Not yet."

"Do you think she will?"

"I really hope so."

"Don't wait much longer..."

"I won't," I said. "If I don't hear from her in the next day or so, I'll move forward with the other applicants."

It had been 16 days and there had been no word from the chick on the boat. I had scheduled four interviews for this morning, hoping to find at least two more staff. I knew the time waiting for the boat to arrive had ended.

A morning rush had started to develop at the cafe. From the moment we unlocked the doors at 5:30 a.m. until just before

10:00 a.m., there was a steady stream of customers. We had already noticed a handful of regulars. The success of a café is greatly determined by the number of "regular" customers. Great cafés will have eight hundred plus customers go through the doors every day. It takes a lot of "regular" customers to make that happen.

In the coffee world, customers are typically known by what they drink well before they are known by name. Although they will never admit it, what a customer orders on a regular basis gives a barista insight into their personal life. It's our crystal ball that doesn't show us the future, rather reveals one's hidden secrets. There are the uncomplicated true coffee purists who stick with black coffee, straight espresso, and unflavored cappuccinos and lattes. These pureists are admired. They are the true coffee connoisseurs.

Once a second ingredient is added to any coffee, it stops being coffee and turns in to a beverage. The more additions, the less it can be considered coffee. As the difficulty of the beverage increases, so does the pretentiousness of the consumer. And no barista will ever understand those customers who order skinny anything to drink with their five hundred calorie scone.

Our customers enjoyed a variety of coffee and were showing signs that they were developing a new habit, and we were it. At 6:00 a.m. sharp, the ex-large dark roast with a bran muffin mortgage broker arrived in his suit and tie. He had a long commute, and we were his first stop. When he showed up on the weekend with his kids, we didn't recognize him.

If the ex-large mocha with extra whipped cream and a slice of lemon bread hadn't arrived by 6:15 a.m., we knew she wasn't on duty at the NIC Unit at the hospital. With each visit, she would tell us of the newest little arrivals and kept us updated on their progress. My youngest daughter had spent a few days in the NIC Unit, so we had a special bond. When she told us of the NIC units exciting successes, I felt them right along with her.

Our large Americano with an extra shot and chocolate croissant Insurance Agent showed up around 7:00 a.m. It didn't take long for him to meet his co-worker each morning, and by week three, half his office showed up before heading in for their morning meeting. I suggested that they have their meetings on the patio, and to my delight that is exactly where they met every Tuesday morning.

At 7:30 a.m., the Chi Latte Biology Teacher arrived; on the weekends he ordered a small coffee. He and his partner were bikers. They ended their weekend rides at the Inkwell.

We served an extra hot regular latte with an extra shot, made with whole milk, to the Engineering Professor from the local college at 8:00 a.m. Some days he ordered two, taking one back for his assistant.

An interesting man began to appear around 8:05 a.m. No one was sure when he started coming or if he had been there from day one. He was of average height, average looks, and wore a light brown coat. The daily order was a medium coffee. It's likely that he would never have been noticed except for the fact he was standing at the counter at 8:05 a.m. "every" morning. Each morning he ordered his coffee, paid with cash, and sat by the window reading the paper until 8:45 a.m. at which time he would leave the store without a word, simply disappearing. He became the invisible man.

After noticing this intriguing gentleman, I took up the challenge to find out more about him.

"How's your morning?" I'd asked.

"Fine," would be the reply.

"Would you like to try a muffin, they're fresh out of the oven?" I would offer.

"No,"

"Busy day today?" I'd ask.

"Typical," was the answer.

Then one morning, I was prepared with what I thought was the question that would get him to say more than two words....

"So, what do you do?" I asked with my most interested smile.

"Not much," was the response which came without an interested smile. Taking his coffee and walking over to his table, he sat down, and opened the paper. At 8:45 a.m., he closed his paper, took a final sip of coffee, and made his way to the door.

"See you tomorrow," I said.

He nodded.

"All right, it's official," I said to the team once he was out the door. "Whoever can break the code and figure out who the invisible man is wins employee of the year!"

"What do we win?" asked Katie, the high school student who learned that rarely does anyone actually win something during such contests.

"You can have free drinks while you're working!" I said with enthusiasm.

"Don't we get that anyway?" she asked.

"Yes, you do! You're a smart one," I said tapping my temples. "I can always spot the smart ones." She smiled, and I walked into the back room.

At 9:55 a.m., the back door swung open and a voice rang out, "Your 10:00 a.m. interview is here."

"Thanks," I said. "9:55 a.m., I love it. Early, that's a good sign." I grabbed the stack of files from the desk and headed out to the patio. As I passed the bar, I placed my order, "My regular, please." I chose my favorite table in the corner, put down the pile of folders, my note tablet and pen, and I made my way back to the bar. Standing with her back to me was a stout young woman observing the activity behind the counter. She had black hair cut in a bob and wore thick black framed glasses. I assumed she was in her mid-twenties.

"Hello," I said holding out my hand. "I'm Jenn, you must be…"

"I'm Rebecca," she said instantly. She had a warm, inviting smile. We shook hands, she had a solid grip. If an applicant's hand is squishy, I'm not the right manager for them.

"What can I get you to drink?" I offered.

"Katie's already getting me something," she said grinning with delight.

"Something good, I hope," I said.

"I'm sure it will be," she said.

Rebecca's Vanilla Latte and my two shots of espresso with a pump of simple syrup over ice, were called out. We took our beverages and wandered out to the patio. Along the way, I pointed out the roaster, the bakery, and our lovely fireplace. We then sat down at the table, and I opened her file.

"So, how do you know Katie?" I asked. She had just taken a sip of her coffee which was hotter than expected. She reached for a napkin and put it up to her mouth. "It's hot, sorry about that."

"No, I knew it was, just couldn't wait to taste it. I don't know Katie, just met her when I came in," she said. "She has a great smile." She patted her lips again.

"She does. This is her first job," I said. "I love first job people, gives me a chance to mold them without having to deal with all the garbage that comes with past jobs and bad managers." I was rolling my hands together and grinning like Dr. Frankenstein just prior to bringing his monster to life. "I get just a little passionate," I said taking back control of my hands and folding them, then placing them on the table. "Do you enjoy talking to strangers?"

"I do!" she said with sincerity. "That's how I met my husband."

"Was he strange or a stranger?"

"Both!" she said with a grin. "I was filling my gas tank, and he was on the other side of the island filling his. I asked him how his day was going and now we're married." She held up her left hand which revealed a modest diamond and band as proof.

"How long have you been together?"

"Married for three years, but he moved in a few weeks after we met," Rebecca said raising her eyebrow, which made me think there was much more to the story.

"That's fast," thinking of my own daughter who was only a few years, or moments, away from the possibility of this same situation.

"Our parents thought so, but they're good with it all now. We're going this weekend to see his folks."

"Do they live close?"

"About three hours," she said. She paused and took another sip of her latte. "I want to take our dogs, but one of them just doesn't get along with their cow."

I reached for my cup, as I brought the straw to my mouth, I said, "Their cow?" I sipped my coffee and held onto the straw. I did my best to control myself; I had a sudden urge to burst into laughter. "Please tell me more."

"I just don't think they'll get along," she said so matter-of-factly.

"Is the cow in the house?" I asked, picturing old Betsy walking around the kitchen.

"No. But my dog gets really protective, and I think he'll try to attack the cow."

I put my cup down and leaned forward. "You have to explain this to me," I said. "Is the cow close to the house? No barn? I come from the Midwest. I've seen cows, but they were in large groups out in the field. I don't ever recall seeing one in someone's backyard." I started outlining boxes on the table with my finger, wanting her to draw me a map.

"She's in their backyard with the goats, but they have a huge back yard."

Goats! Where am I? Either she's making this up or... I don't know?

She continued, "Sometimes they are close to the house, and sometimes they are by the back fence. There's no way to separate them."

"I see," I said nodding my head. "Sounds like an interesting place to visit." Suddenly, the oddities that came with visiting my own parents and in-laws seemed incosequential. "Do you visit often?"

"Not really," she said.

"I guess I can see why," I said.

"It's just too complicated," she said.

"No kidding."

We laughed, drank coffee, and talked for almost an hour, and I was greatly relieved that the cows and the dogs and the in-laws were the only bizarre part of our conversation. We were interrupted by the announcement that my 11:00 a.m. interview had arrived. We said goodbye, and I walked back to the counter to introduce myself to my next candidate.

There is protocol to interviewing. Companies typically have a list of questions that are required to be asked of every candidate. I recall my first few interviews where I felt forced to focus on the questions. Asking the questions wasn't bad, it was the writing of the answers that screwed me up. I never really heard the person's responses because I was more concerned with how I would write them down. It didn't take me long to realize I'm not a form filling interviewer. I rarely follow script anymore. I like to hear stories because in those stories are who the person really is. Becca was fun, she was friendly, she anticipated issues, sought ways to avoid potential problems, and she's a risk-taker. And if I ever had a cow and invited her to come over, she would think twice before bringing her dogs.

The interviews went on for a few more hours. In the middle of the last one, my Roaster walked over and announced, "She's here."

"Who's here?" I asked.

"The boat chick," she said.

"Really?"

"Yep, she's waiting for a drink," she pointed towards the bar.

"I'll be right over," I said. "Please tell her to have a seat."

I watched as the Roaster walked back toward the bar. Standing there was a woman in a black business suit, heels, and a Michael Kors handbag flung over her shoulder; a far cry from the windblown, dry cleaning carrying traveler I had met a few weeks ago. After the Roaster relayed my message, the woman turned, smiled, and waved with the excitement that equaled seeing an old friend after a long absence.

I did my best to finish the current interview and offer the slightest notion that I was still engaged in our conversation. I ended it quickly, walked him to the door, and thanked him for coming in. Then I made my way over to the high top table Suzie had chosen. I reached out my hand and she said, "Hi, I'm Suzie. I'm here to talk to you about a job..."

Terms Used to Describe Coffee

Beans from different countries or regions have distinctive characteristics in their **_flavor, aroma, body, and acidity._** These taste characteristics are dependent not only on the coffee's growing region, but also on genetic subspecies (varietals) and processing.

8 | The 10 Alarm Lattes

"It's good to see you," I said. "Your drink OK? Can I get you anything else?" I looked at the side of the cup, she was a soy vanilla latte.

"My drink is divine," she said. "We serve great coffee here."

"Yes, we do," I agreed. I slid onto the stool and laid my files on the table. "How was your trip?"

"It was awesome. The weather was perfect. They have a new captain," she said in a tone that suggested I many have known the old one.

"How does that work?" I asked, unfamiliar with yachts, captains, and the latest issue of the Yachting Monthly. "I only have a father-in-law with a speed boat that no one but he is allowed to drive. Is there like a pool of captains who wait to get hired for specific trips?" I was envisioning a line of Popeye the Sailor Men standing on a long dock waving their hands in the air waiting to be chosen.

"No, it's his full-time job." By the way she nodded her head, I knew this wasn't her maiden voyage.

"Really? Do they live on the boat?"

"No, but he could. It's big enough."

"What does he do when they aren't sailing?" I asked.

"Keeps the boat up, scrapes barnacles off the bottom." She laughed and brushed her bangs back. "He asked if I would like to stay and help him scrape barnacles."

"Tempting?" I asked. If she wasn't tempted, I was considering sending my application.

"No, I'm not the barnacle type. I'd much rather be sitting on the deck drinking margaritas."

"Wouldn't we all," I said. "So, tell me about yourself."

"I live with my dad, he needs a little assistance."

"That's cool. How old is he?"

"Almost 70."

"And your mom?"

"She died when I was little."

"I'm so sorry. That had to be tough." I felt horrible, but Suzie had a way about her that was so a-matter-of-fact yet calming that I instantly felt we were best friends, and she had taken me into her confidence. I had never met anyone like her.

"Yeah, it was a lot for my dad, so some of us went to live with our aunts in the south for a few years."

"So that's where your accent is from."

"Do you think I have an accent?" she said truly surprised.

"You've never heard that before?" She just looked at me. "Yes, you have a tiny southern drawl mixed in there." She smiled. "I lived in the south for eight years, I know southern drawl." She grinned and shook her head. Now, I didn't know if she was joking or telling the truth. "So, back to your dad."

"He's getting older and I don't have a family, so we just started living together a while back."

"That's great that he still gets around."

"Yeah. He lost a leg many years ago..." Again, she just blurted it out as if she was telling me she had an apple tree in her back yard.

"He what?" It wasn't that I hadn't heard of such a thing; I had never heard anyone speak of such a thing so matter-of-factly.

"He lost a leg a long time ago. Being one-legged has just been a way of life. We kids don't really think about it. But as he is getting older, it's a little more difficult getting around.

"Oh, I can imagine," I offered.

"He has a handicap parking permit, but I don't let him use it." Once again, I was blindsided by this conversation.

"You don't? I would think he qualifies."

"'No.' I tell him," she said shaking her finger at me, "'that's meant for people who have a real disability, you can walk.'" I wasn't sure how to respond. "The worst is when we have to buy shoes, they're so flippin' expensive."

"I can imagine." Although, I had never really thought about it.

"And we have to buy two. What's up with that?" Suzie waved two fingers in the air. " They're made specially, don't you think they could just make one?"

"Sounds reasonable to me." Oh, the education I'm getting today... Cows and dogs, one-legged fathers...

"No. Two." She held up her fingers proving the amount. "I just threw out a box full of brand new left shoes. No reason keeping them, it's not like his leg's going to grow back." Feeling it may not be appropriate, I concentrated on the subject at hand in hopes it would allow me not to laugh. It was the second bizarre conversation I'd had so far this day, but this one was quickly passing the cow and dogs and in-laws.

"Can't find someone who needs one left shoe?" I asked, hoping not to offend.

"I've tried."

"I bet you have."

"I have," she said with eyebrows raised.

"I believe you!" I said, shaking my head emphatically.

"No takers." She took another sip of coffee. "This is good."

"I'm glad you like it," I said taking a deep breath and relieved to change the subject. "If it wasn't, we wouldn't be doing our job. Let's get back to the job...why coffee? Why here?"

"I think it would be a hoot," she said. "I love talking to people. I'm a decent salesperson, and I love the atmosphere." She looked around the café, smiled and waved to a couple coming in from the patio.

"Do you know them?" I asked.

"Nope." She said with no further explanation.

Good Lord, I'm sitting with Dolly Levy!

We talked for about twenty more minutes when I unexpectedly looked up at her and said, "This isn't typical, not even appropriate, but I think you can handle it. I'm sure you would be a real addition to our store. I would also like the opportunity to work with you. If you're still interested, would you like to fill out the paperwork today? You might as well get paid for your time."

"Sure!" she said.

I went to the back room and retrieved the new hire folder with training material and returned to the table. Suzie sat there filling in her tax information, and I began mapping out her training.

"Do you have any ID with you, like a driver's license, passport, social security card? I need to prove you're not an alien."

"I've been trying to keep my antennas down," she said reaching back to get her purse. "I have a passport."

"You carry that with you?"

"Sure, never know when I'll need it."

"Do you find the need to leave the country often?"

"Not typically, but if the need would ever arise, I don't want to have to go home first."

"Makes sense." I said, nodding and shaking my head at the same time. In less than an hour, I've had enough insight of this person that I would not doubt an invitation to leave the country could come at any moment; or she does something so bizarre that leaving the country would be her only option. Either way, I was intrigued. "This is all I need," taking the passport from her.

Suzie rubbed her hand along her arm. "As far as being an alien, I've found that wearing a suit helps to hide the scales."

"That it does," I said. "Works to hide the green skin as well." I flipped my cuff up to reveal my scales.

"Dark colors are always best," she smiled and gave me the thumbs up.

I began filling out the I-9 Form when I realized there was added commotion around the coffee roaster. Out of the corner of my eye, I saw a blue flashing light.

"Excuse me," I said.

"5 Alarm Latte," echoed through the store. In an instant, doors were opened and manned, the Roaster was fanning the smoke and spraying cold water on the overly heated beans, and I had the phone in my hand. Three minutes later, we heard the sirens in the distance. I stood next to the barista assisting in the final prep of the lattes when I heard, "What can I do to help?" Suzie was on the other side of me, apron on, hands washed, and ready for action.

"You can put these in a carrying tray, I think we better go ahead and make five more. We can always give them away if we have any left over. I'm going to talk to the guests."

Suzie took the lattes that were finished and placed them in the drink carrier. She set a second one up for the next batch, then I watched as she began to walk table by table on the opposite side of the café talking to guests, assuring them that everything was all right.

The sirens got closer and to our regret, five vehicles pulled up. "Apparently, they send everyone," I said. Ten uniformed officers entered the store. I introduced myself and walked them to the roaster. "I'm sorry I didn't get to you in time." I said.

"Not a problem," the chief said. "Better safe than sorry."

I explained our alarm system and what the in-house procedures were. "I'll try harder to get to the phone faster," I promised.

"Would you boys like a drink?" I heard from behind me. "Gotta love a man in uniform!" Suzie handed each a latte as she read their names off their badges. "I'll be here every morning, I expect to see you before you start your shift. Actually, before, during, and after would be just fine." Her southern twang became very apparent when she said "just fine."

The ten officers followed me as I led them through the store. They were genuinely interested as they checked the dates on the fire extinguishers we passed, and double-checked the connections for the sprinkler systems.

"When would the sprinklers turn on?" one of them asked.

"It's all timed," I said. "Next to the blue warning light is the sprinkler delay. The Roast Master has the power to disconnect the sprinklers if there isn't a fire. If our alarm ever goes off and you don't receive a call, you can be sure it's not beans and the place is likely going up in flames.

"Good to know," another said.

"Can I get anyone anything else?" Suzie asked, as she sashayed into the back room. "Michael," she said pointing to the youngest of the men, "you need a chocolate chip cookie to go with that latte?"

"No, we're good," a slightly red faced officer said.

The parade of officers exited the store, and as they returned to their vehicles, Suzie yelled out, "Let me know anytime you're bored and I'll try my hand at roasting!" They all laughed, started their engines, and five emergency vehicles exited the parking lot.

When I returned to the counter, I was handed the phone.

"So, how many lattes is it?" Gregg asked.

"Ten," I said. "Apparently, you get the alarm as well."

"Yep, part of the job."

"Nice to know you're keeping an eye on us," I replied a bit relieved that he didn't seem overly concerned.

"I'll be over your way next week."

"Good," I said. "We've got some new faces."

"I'm looking forward to it."

"Anything else?" I asked.

"No. Should there be?" he replied.

"No. Not if we're doing what is expected of us."

"No complaints on this end," he said.

"Thanks for checking in, Gregg. Next time I'll get to the phone quicker."

"Not too much quicker. We've found that the attention all those officers bring to a store isn't all bad for business."

"Wow, that's a very clever marketing gimmick."

"It ain't cheap, but very effective."

"Interesting."

Americano

An Americano is the desired number of espresso shots and water. This can be served hot or cold. Flavor profile varies whether shots are added to water or water is added to shots. Can also be made by pouring espresso shots over ice and adding water.

The drink "Americano" comes from when American GIs in WWII would order their espresso with water because it was too strong.

9 | Taking Orders

Summer was rapidly approaching and with it came tourists and summer vacation. My daughter had arranged an intern position for her little brother, so neither of our kids would be home for the summer. Although I would miss the summer explorations we were known for, I knew how exhausting it would be to have a summer filled with adventures after expending all my energy at the café. A quiet summer would be just fine this year.

As Daniel and I sat on the balcony watching the sunset, he asked, "Want to go anywhere on your day off? You are getting a day off, aren't you?"

"Yes and No."

"Yes what,"

"Yes, I'm getting a day off, and no I don't need to go anywhere."

"You sure?"

"Yep! I talk more in a day than most people do in a week. Between my customers, the team, and now Suzie and Becca, I will be very happy doing nothing. Quiet sounds good!"

"Good," he replied raising his pint glass filled with *hoppyness.*

"It's all good," I said raising my party glass to the sun.

My interview day had been very successful as I acquired both Rebecca and Suzie. Over the next three weeks, both ladies had finished their assigned reading and classroom part of their training and were ready to get behind the counter. In this very short time, both had established themselves quite securely within the store.

Suzie had a story for any subject that was mentioned. With each story came the realization that not only had she lived a very interesting life, but she found humor everywhere. Her delivery was impeccable. Rebecca, or as she preferred to be called, Becca, had the gift of gab, and she used it to its fullest. Between the two, no one could get a word in and no one really needed to. Watching the two of them was like watching a Saturday Night Live sketch, only funnier.

I had decided to train both on the register at the same time. "Training screws up the entire flow of the store, so why not get it all over with quickly," I recalled myself saying when I made the schedule. It was 8:55 a.m. when the register training was about to begin that I began regretting my decision.

Ten minutes later, my new recruits stood at attention with clean aprons and big smiles. "Ready?" I asked.

"Yes!" Replied Becca confidently.

"Sure," said Suzie—looking not as confident.

"When you take an order," I began, "you have to think as a barista thinks."

"But I'm not a barista," Suzie said.

"I know, but you have to think like one." I looked for some sign indicating she understood.

Suzie stood at attention, swiped her hand in front of her face; with the swipe, her expression changed, "I am a barista!" She said overenunciating.

I bit my lip to keep from laughing. "So, let's think about it. What is the first detail a barista needs to know before they can make a drink?"

"The size!" Becca blurted out.

"Before that?" I asked. They both looked at me blankly.

"Hot or cold," a voice replied from behind the bar.

"Thanks," I said. "That's right. We have to know if we are making a hot or iced drink. To prevent us from having to say "hot" all the time, we assume it's hot unless you say "iced." For example, you don't say hot coffee or hot mocha. You would only differentiate if it were to be made iced. What's the second detail we need to know?" I cued Becca in that now was the time to give her previous answer.

"Size!" Becca said again.

"Correct!" I said. "Next is the amount of espresso shots, followed by the type of milk, followed by any sweeteners, and finally toppings. Fortunately, our registers think like a barista and that is the order of the prompts. It may seem confusing at the beginning, but once you learn the sequence for taking orders, you'll also know the order for making the drinks."

"Brilliant," Becca said.

"Yeah, remember that I'm not a barista?" Suzie said pointing her finger at me.

Pointing back at her, "Don't worry, I'm not going to make you work the bar until you're ready," I assured her.

"Which will never happen," she announced.

The barista laughed, "That would probably be best," he said.

"Hey!" Suzie snapped. "I don't know if I like you--or hate you--because of that statement. I'll let you know when I decide."

"Back to our training," I said attempting to bring the conversation back. I had learned over the past few weeks that these two could find endless distractions and tangents. I did my best to keep a short leash on them but this required me to hold on tightly. It was like walking puppies; they chase anything that moves, smell anything with a scent, and lay down in the middle of the sidewalk when they are tired.

I had learned the tight leash trick when Becca and Suzie went to training classes together. The trainer commented on how interesting they made the classes. It was never described as a negative interruption, just that the trainer felt as if he lost total control and found that these two somehow began to guide him through the training. Each call always ended with the same comments, "I think they'll be great, good luck managing them."

"Back to our training," I suggested. "Let's just worry about the registers for now. For the next few minutes, I want you to stand behind the two working the register and observe. Listen to the orders given and watch how they enter them. Remember, we don't expect our customers to order the way we enter their drinks. They can say it anyway they like, it's your job to put it in the correct order when entering it into the register."

"But if we did teach them how to order," Becca began.

"Then I would have them order and I wouldn't have to pay you," I said. Suzie was wide-eyed as she buttoned her lip.

"True," Becca replied.

"Time to observe--ten minutes--listen, watch, and learn. And DON'T leave your spots." I placed my hands on Becca's shoulders and placed her next to the far register. "Stand right here." I then did the same with Suzie, who carefully placed her feet inside one square of tile. She then saluted me. "Don't move," I said again.

Less than 30 seconds later Becca had asked her training buddy if she could take over, and Suzie was already lost in conversation with the customers. "A nightmare, this is going to be a nightmare. Why don't I hire normal people?" I mutted, shaking my head.

"Hey!" the barista said.

"Oh, did I say that out loud? Well, if you don't know by now, everyone on this team is just a little off. But I'm sure there's counseling for that - I doubt it would help."

"No," he said. "It didn't."

"I'm sorry," I said placing my hand on his shoulder. "We'll love you as long as you keep making those perfect lattes."

"A perfect Soy Latte and a perfect Mocha," he called out to the next customers.

I allowed the two trainees to have it their way for the next five minutes. They appeared confident so I forced their hand. Each stepped up to their prospective registers and began taking orders. I was amazed how quickly comfortable Becca was after the second order. It was boggling to watch the fun-loving, confident, Suzie begin to shake and sweat. I stood behind her for the next hour, guiding her through each transaction and adding as much levity as possible with each order.

"Don't worry," I said. "It takes more and more time to get comfortable with registers if you're over the age of thirty. We didn't grow up playing on computers. It doesn't come naturally."

"Do you think I'm over 30?" Suzie snapped.

"No! I don't think you are but your passport does. You don't look a day over 25!" I said.

"Right answer," Suzie assured. "We're going to work well together."

By the end of the shift, Suzie had conquered her fears and found ways to overcompensate for her lack of speediness by joking about it. For the next week, she told every customer it was her first day. And for those who knew better and refused to buy her excuses, she somehow turned the lack of speed back on them.

By the end of the week, they were pros and ready to take on the morning rush. Halfway through their first early morning shift, a familiar face walked through the front door. He smiled, nodded to them, and then began to walk through the store. He stopped at the roaster. While gazing at the coffee being churned in the cooling bin, he reached in and picked up a bean, popped it in his mouth and began crunching. As the Roaster watched, he nodded his head and moved on.

He looked at the tables and chairs as if inspecting them after all, he was. It was Gregg, and he was doing what was known as the Gregg Walk. He would inspect the entire store before making introductions or having conversations. I realized that he had stopped at the fireplace and was fiddling with something. He moved on to the patio and then through the bakery. Eventually, he was standing next to the espresso machine.

"Welcome," I said.

"Thanks."

"Take you long to get here?" I asked.

"No, not really."

"What are you drinking?" I offered.

"Let's do a three shot Americano," he said.

"Nice," the barista said.

"Has no effect anymore," he said. "New faces up front?"

"Our star pupils. I'll introduce you."

I introduced him to Suzie and Becca and left him engulfed in endless conversation, while I went to see what he had been doing by the fireplace. On a small ledge just above the opening, I saw my name written in the dust. I laughed and walked back to the counter.

It was entertaining to watch him struggle to escape the endless chatter from Suzie and Becca. Finally pulling himself from the sea of words, he picked up his drink, and we walked into the back room.

"I see you've learned to spell my name," I said.

"Sure have. Did you erase it?" He asked.

"No, I thought you were labeling it so I knew it was mine." I said.

"Very funny."

"Couldn't find anything else wrong, so you had to pick out a few pieces of dust above the fireplace, a working fireplace, need I remind you."

"That's how I roll," he said proudly.

"Thanks. I take great pride in knowing that the only issue is that there is dust above my working fireplace."

"You should," he said.

"Anything else?" I asked.

"I've got some reports for you. We can sit down out front and go over them. We're growing faster than planned. Your budget has been realigned to match the new projections."

"Not a bad problem to have," I said. "I like my little world."

"Remember, your little world is in my universe."

"Yes, sir."

"We've got a spill on aisle three!" Suzie announced as she threw open the back door. It slammed against the back wall.

"I've got to get a doorstopper back here. Some day that door's going through to the next store. We'll be able to sell swimsuits through the hole."

"Is that what's next door?"

"Haven't you noticed? Welcome to life at the beach!"

"Gotta get the mop!" Suzie interrupted, as she squeezed through the crowded back room making her way to the mop sink in the back corner. She dropped the mop into the filled bucket and began rolling it to the front. "Excuse me, pardon me," she said rolling directly toward Gregg, who stepped back against the shelves and put his hands up as if being arrested. Suzie didn't notice. She continued, "Some customers need sippy cups. Oh, what a mess they've made. Don't worry--I'm on it!"

"I'm sure you are," I said, as she slammed though the door making it hit the large coffee cabinet that sat just outside. I glanced up to see Gregg's questioning expression. "I'll make sure everything's all right," I said.

"I think it's best," he said.

I entered the café to see Becca mopping the floor and Suzie drying Bob off. Bob was a regular. He was a tall, scruffy man with a minimum of teeth. He was never clean-shaven, there was always stubble. It seemed as if he shaved; not close enough to be called shaved, yet enough to look like it was trimmed. He wore old t-shirts with logos that had vanished years ago.

Bob usually ordered a large coffee and stood by the Espresso Bar talking to the barista and other guests for about an hour. We didn't know Bob's story, but knew that he needed to stand at our pick-up counter and talk to anyone about anything. It was his daily routine. Bob was a constant reminder that for many of our customers, we were the bartender without alcohol. We were their "other" place. We were their "Cheers!"

"Now, Bob," I heard Suzie say, "If you can't handle a big boy cup, I'll have to put your coffee in a sippy, you don't want that now, do you?" Bob was grinning from ear to ear, loving every minute of it. "Becca, there's some coffee on the floor way over there." Suzie pointed, flinging her towel in the air, and Becca dutifully mopped in that direction.

"You must be more careful Robert, it's a good thing this nice little lady didn't get coffee on her new blue shoes." Suzie said as she stopped to admire the shoes of the customer who was next in line. "Look at those shoes!" Suzie leaned back and rested against Bob's arm. Waving her towel in the air, she said, "Honey, where did you get them?" Suzie stood with her hand on her chin admiring the shoes.

The blue shoe lady looked down at her shoes and told Suzie where they were purchased, how much they cost, the event they were purchased for, how many people were at the event, how she had come upon the tickets for the event, the number of compliments she had received at the event. She pulled out her phone. "I'll give them a call right now and see if they have them in your size," she offered.

"No, no, no, don't bother, but thanks for offering," Suzie said tapping her toe to draw attention to the black, non-slip, closed toe, food service approved, not exciting shoes she was wearing.

By this time, Gregg was standing next to me. We both watched the performance. The next customer in line offered to buy Bob a coffee to replace the one that spilled.

"No worries, deary," Suzie said. "It's on the house, but if you're buying, I'm sure the lady behind you wouldn't mind."

Without hesitation he turned, asked what she was drinking, and put it on his tab. I watched. I could do nothing else. My already very friendly café had just been pushed over the top. Suzie had taken what would have been a naturally embarrassing situation and turned it into an event. Suddenly, we had strangers talking to each other, buying each other drinks, and Bob was pleased as could be that he was the center of attention.

"Where did you find her?" Gregg whispered.

"She just flew in, kinda like Mary Poppins." I said.

"Can you find ten more?" he asked.

"Don't think the world could handle ten of them."

"You're probably right," he said.

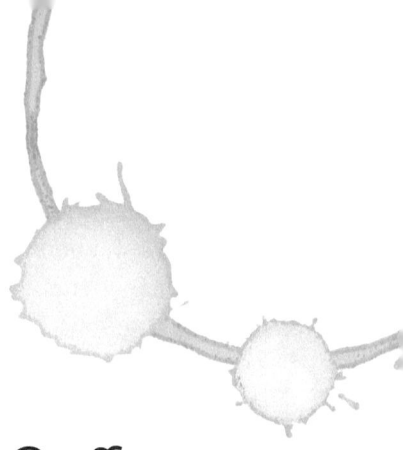

Decaffeinated Coffee

Decaffeination is the process of removing caffeine from coffee beans. Since coffee contains an estimated 400 different chemicals that contribute to its overall flavor and aromatic qualities, the goal of decaffeination is to leave these valuable chemicals intact while removing the one undesirable chemical, caffeine.

Decaffeination of coffee beans may be accomplished through the direct contact method or the indirect contact method of decaffeination.

The indirect contact method of decaffeination, chemicals (other than water) are used on green coffee beans (milled but not yet roasted) with the goal of dissolving and extracting the caffeine.

The direct contact decaffeination method uses chemicals with the coffee beans and also may utilize supercritical carbon dioxide, which is carbon dioxide stored at a high pressure and temperature so it may be used as a decaffeination agent.

10 | Mission - The Invisible Man

The following week Suzie took her position as an opener and was permanently entered on the schedule for the opening shifts. When I pulled into the parking lot a few minutes before 5 a.m., she was already standing at the door with as much energy as I had ever seen her have. We entered the store together and began the tasks at hand. At 5:25 a.m., we met at the bar for our power drink, toasted the day, and unlocked the door.

"Try to get your first sale in before 5:30 a.m." I said.

"OK, but why?" she asked.

"It's a payroll trick," I said. "We are allowed payroll hours based on our customer counts. If we can have one sale before 5:30 a.m., we actually earn additional payroll. It's a win win! The customer wins because we opened early, and we win because we get a few extra hours."

"Good plan," she said giving me her trademark thumbs-up.

We had quadrupled our regulars since those first few weeks. The 6:00 a.m. ex-large dark roast with a bran muffin, Mortgage Broker, showed up every weekday. The ex-large mocha, with extra whip cream and six donut holes, now required a carrier to take the additional four drinks she picked up for her fellow NICU co-workers, along with the box of pastries. Our large Americano, with an extra shot and chocolate croissant, Insurance Agent, showed up around 7:00 a.m. and met most of his clients here during the day. The 7:30 a.m. Chi Latte, Biology Teacher, began changing his order and took great pleasure in making us guess what he was having on any given day. And by 8:00 a.m., the extra hot regular latte, with an extra shot made with whole milk, Engineering Professor, was now called by his first name, Phil.

After Phil had ordered, I told Suzie about the invisible man.

"Where is he?" she asked.

"He's invisible," I said. "And he's not here yet, you'll know him when you see him. Try to get some information. We can't get him to say more than two words."

"What's his name?" she asked.

"Haven't got a clue."

"What does he do?"

"Don't know."

"Maybe he's a spy," she said.

"A spy who spends every morning in our café?"

"Why not, we have some very interesting customers," she said mysteriously.

"And employees," I said.

"GOOD MORNING!" Suzie greeted the next customer who was wearing a very familiar brown coat.

"Medium coffee," he said.

"How about a blueberry muffin with that?" she asked.

"No thanks."

"Got a busy day planned?" she asked.

"Just average," he said.

"So, what do you do?" Suzie asked with great excitement.

"Work," he said.

She turned to me, "Jenn, get a cup of coffee for this customer named...." we waited for him to fill in the blank... Silence. "....for our customer who works," she said finishing the transaction.

As she handed him his change, she locked eyes with him. "I'm on to you," she said. "I'll keep it a secret that you're an international spy who uses our café to receive secret messages through our coffee. It'll be our little secret."

I couldn't hold back. I burst into laughter. The invisible man squinted slightly; I saw the corner of his mouth twitch just a bit. He picked up his coffee, nodded, took his usual seat, and opened his paper. I kept one eye on him for the remainder of the hour he was there. On several occasions, I saw him sneak a peek at the party that was happening behind the counter. "Mr. Banks, I believe you've met your Mary Poppins," I said as I watched him.

A few minutes later I heard, "It's your birthday!!" Standing in front of Suzie was a businessman dressed in a suit and tie. "Birthdays are special here at the Inkwell!" she said.

They are? I thought.

Suzie picked up the phone and pressed 5. "Hey, baker man, do we have any brownies or cupcakes back there for a birthday? There's got to be some leftovers. I'm guessing this guy doesn't have anything planned, and I feel sorry for him." The customer began to blush. "We do, bring it on up. If you can find a candle, that would be great! Just one--if we used the correct amount, the fire department would show up," and she hung up the phone.

"Let's all sing," she raised her hand to conduct the chorus of customers standing in front of her. "Happy birthday..." To my amazement, they all were singing. As I scanned the café, several guests had turned in their chairs and were providing additional voices. As they finished the song, the Baker came around the corner with a plate containing a large brownie piled high with whipped cream. He handed it to Suzie, who in turn handed it across the counter. "There's no candle," she said, as she wrinkled her nose and shook her head. "But don't say anything, 'he's,'" she pointed to the Baker, "a little sensitive."

The birthday boy took the plate, smiled, and nodded. "Now remember," Suzie said. "My birthday--you're going to want to right this down." She pointed out to her audience as if directing them to grab their calendars. "My birthday is in February, go on write it down, you won't want to forget... February. Don't worry, you have time. I'll be reminding you as it gets closer."

I watched as the birthday boy took his brownie and coffee and headed towards a table. The café was filled with birthday wishes. Then, I remembered the invisible man... I glanced over. For the first time ever, his paper was lying on the table, he was sitting back in his chair with his arms crossed, watching the whole production. "Oh, she's breaking him down."

Theodore Roosevelt Drank a Ton of Coffee!

This is not an exaggeration: Teddy was known to drink a gallon of coffee a day. No wonder he was able to get so much done in the wake of the American Civil War!

Teddy is noted to have helped Maxwell House come up with their famous slogan, 'Good Till The Last Drop'. He actually came up with that slogan while drinking coffee in Andrew Jackson's living room!

11 | A Troubled Well

June rolled into July, and we rolled merrily along.

The Fourth of July brought thousands of tourists to our little town, and I was convinced that they all got their coffee at the Inkwell. As the tourists arrived, our regulars began taking vacations but never left before informing us of their plans, as not to worry us when they didn't show up for a week or two. Upon their return, there were endless stories and pictures of their adventures.

Each day seemed to bring us new regular customers. There were two men in particular who had all our attention. The first was a charming young plastic surgeon doing his internship just outside Beverly Hills. He was the first person who could shut Suzie up with his stories. Dr. Steve visited the café several times throughout the day. None of us had used his services so we couldn't say whether he was good or not, but according to him, he was the best.

The second was a rugged looking character. He wore blue jeans, boots, perfectly pressed button down shirts and always with a sweater or vest. He arrived around 8:00 a.m. each morning, ordered a cup of coffee in a ceramic mug. He then settled into a leather chair beside the fireplace. He would pull out a pad of paper and a pen from his worn leather satchel and begin writing. Around 11:00 a.m., he would get up, visit the restroom, get a refill of his coffee, and return to his chair.

This happened again around 1:00 p.m. and again at 3:00 p.m. After the third day of this routine, I sent the Magic Maker out to investigate.

She sat with him for a short time and then reported back, "He's writing a screenplay."

"Really?" I asked.

"Yup, sounds like a big deal."

"But he's actually handwriting it?" I asked.

"I asked him that. He prefers handwriting it and then has an assistant put it on the computer."

"His assistant? Maybe he's for real!" We had lots of writers who visited the store on a regular basis, but to date, we hadn't encountered one who actually made a real living at it. "Did he tell you what it's about?"

"No, couldn't get any of that out of him."

"Maybe it's all about us!" Suzie said blowing a puff of air onto her finger nails and wiping them on her shirt.

"Yes, I'm sure he is writing down every detail of our exciting adventures," I said.

"Oh, who will play me?" She asked, resting her hands on her chest.

"Who do you think should play you?" I asked, wanting to see where this story was going.

"Kate Hepburn," she said.

"She's dead," I reminded her.

Suzie placed the back of her hand on her forehead, "Such a shame. A life cut short before she could play the role of a lifetime--ME!"

"She was in her nineties, I don't consider that cutting short." I gave my attention back to the Magic Maker while Suzie got lost in her Academy Award speech. "Did he happen to mention why he sits in our leather chair all day and only buys a cup of coffee?"

"He actually apologized for that. I told him, as long as he mentioned us in his credits, it's ok."

"Nice," I said, "let's hope it isn't porn."

"Do you think there is actually a script for porn?" Suzie's attention immediately returned.

"Never thought about it 'till this very minute," I said. "Does he have a name?"

"Michael...Michael the screenplay writer."

Michael showed up every morning, except for Sundays, and spent the day with us.

The following week during a phone conversation, Gregg asked if I would be willing to visit a fellow store manager. "He's really struggling," Gregg said. "He's turned over his entire staff, and sales are nowhere near where they should be.

I just think he's new and inexperienced. If you can get away, I would appreciate it if you could spend a day with him."

I hesitated before committing to the assignment. My store was young and my team still new; it didn't seem smart to pull my attention away. With some additional coaxing, I agreed. *After all, it's only for a day,* I thought.

On the day of my managerial mentoring adventure, I stopped at the café first, got my two shots of espresso over ice with a shot of simple syrup, got back in the car and headed north. There were several Inkwells along the coast, all spaced between an hour to an hour and a half apart. The drive was beautiful. The ocean breeze kept the summer temperatures from blazing, and the views were breathtaking.

I arrived at the struggling café midmorning and walked into an almost deserted store. "Where is everyone?" I asked.

"This is normal for us," the young girl said from behind the counter. She seemed more likely to be entering Jr. High then our acceptable hiring age of 16.

"Yeah, this is normal," another chimed in. A trio of stereotypical pom-pom girls giggled.

I waited for a greeting or offer to get me coffee. I waited 'till I was sure that none of them had any intention of assisting me in any way. Then I walked toward the back of the café.

I chuckled to myself as I realized that I was doing the Gregg Walk, but there was more than dust on the fireplace. Under the tables were several days worth of crumbs. No one was behind the bakery counter which looked filthy. It resembled a set from the Muppets after the Swedish Chef blew something up.

The roaster was covered with dust and ash. I had the urge to write more than a name in it. Surrounding it was one quarter of the expected burlap coffee bags. There were three customers sitting at three very separate tables. Bad eighties music was playing through the speakers in the ceiling. I couldn't recall the last time I heard canned music at my store. We had a waiting list of musicians hoping for a chance to serenade our customers. The bad recorder player would have been better.

The café was cold, empty, and depressing; it was a morgue. The three employees behind the counter were either unaffected or had not noticed my reactions as I walked the store. I returned and stood at the counter waiting again.

"Did you want something?" one of the girls finally asked after finishing a text message on her phone.

"Sure, what do you suggest?"

"I don't drink coffee," she said.

"Really, isn't it difficult to work here?" I asked.

"No," she said. I was convinced she was the Invisible Man's daughter.

The second girl emptied the contents of the blender into a large cup, inserted a straw and took a sip. It was a green concoction which the Inkwell did not have on their menu. "I love this stuff," she said. "I buy it at the health food store. It's really good for you." She set the dirty blender cup down on the counter just hard enough to force some of its remains to fly up and land on the wall. I looked up, there were dried green spots on the ceiling. She walked over to the bakery case and looked in. "We should start making blueberry muffins again."

"I can't stand them," the third girl chimed in.

"I like them. I'm tired of the chocolate croissants." She reached in the case, retrieved and then inspected a croissant. She put it back and took another. Upon finding it acceptable, took a big bite. With drink in one hand and croissant in the other, she made her way around the case and sat down at a table.

I grabbed onto the counter to steady myself, and my fingers were met with hard gobs of gum blanketed with a gooey layer of slim. I cringed yet again without inspecting the sticky substance remaining on my hand and reached for the old towel that was laying in a crumpled filthy mess next to the register. None of the three charming young ladies behind the counter paid any attention to me as they continued to be lost in their own worlds.

"Are you out of blueberry muffins?" I inquired.

"No, just stopped making them. Don't care for them. Hey," she continued, "we've got to call in our lunch order. Josh will bring it over before their rush. We need to get their order ready. I think Rudy's working, so we need to add an iced mocha for his girlfriend."

"Is this a standing order?" I asked.

"More like a trade off. They bring us lunch, and we give them drinks."

"Wow, that's a great system you have," I said. I began looking around the store for the hidden cameras. This couldn't really be happening? Could they be that stupid? This has to be Candid Camera. Maybe Gregg set this all up.

I took a deep breath and interrupted the indepth discussion on which lunch platters they were ordering from the Chinese Restaurant across the street, "I'm Jenn, I manage the Inkwell Café south of here." It was as if I had pulled out a gun and told them to lie down on the ground. They all three went pale. "Is Kenneth here?" I asked.

"He's...." she stopped and looked toward the back door.

"He's busy," another said.

"Did he know you were coming?" the third said from her seat at the table and in a tone suggesting that I should have made an appointment.

"Yes, I believe he did." There was a sudden bang as something hit the back wall. "Is he in the back room?" I asked. There was no reply.

I started walking toward the door, and as I reached out to swing open the door, they shouted in unison, "You can't go back there!"

I stopped, surprised by the statement and unsettled by the tone. "And why not?" I asked. I stood waiting for a response.

"He's not alone."

"What do you mean, *he's not alone*?"

The girl who had been sitting at the table was now standing behind the counter. The three looked at each other and then back at the door--then back at each other again. I followed their glances, waiting to make eye contact with one of them. "When the door is closed and his apron is on the hook," she pointed to the black apron hanging on a hook in the center of the door, "that means we can't go back there, and he's not alone."

"Who's with him?" Silence. "Is he receiving an order?" Their giggles made the hair on the back of my neck stand up. I felt my blood pressure soar. "Why can't I go back there?"

They once again looked at each other. Finally, the girl with a set of keys wrapped around her wrist said, "It's just one of his girls." She shrugged her shoulders as if it was no big deal.

"One of his girls? I hope you don't mean what I think you mean. This happens often?" I asked. They shrugged and giggled some more. I stood at the door listening, hoping I couldn't hear anything. I reached into my bag and grabbed my phone. I could turn on the camera and charge back there, or I could lie and say I have a call. I went with the lie. "I have a call, I'll be right back," I said as I headed for the front door. I left the store, got out of view, and dialed.

"Hello," I heard on the other end.

"Where are you?" I asked.

"Why?" Gregg asked.

"I think you need to get here and get here quickly," I said.

"I'm an hour north. Why? What's going on?" he asked.

"It's a mess, it's a fucking mess. The store is dirty, the children behind the counter are making their own drinks, eating out of the bakery case, and supposedly exchanging drinks for lunch from another restaurant."

"What do you mean, making their own drinks?"

"She brings stuff from home and uses our blenders. That's not the worst, Gregg, shit, I can't even say it."

"What?"

"Apparently," I took a deep breath. My heart was pounding so hard I felt it in my head. "Your manager has a steady stream of customers that he services in the back room."

"He what? What do you mean *services*?"

"He has girls--women--who knows--in the back room. I've stopped my brain from trying to imagine what they do. Oh God, I want to throw up."

"Are you sure?"

My mind was racing. I could barely put my sentences together. I knew it sounded strange. It was strange! It was awful. Why would he believe me? I didn't believe me, and I had just lived it. "Did you ever notice the hook in the center of his back door?"

"He said it's for a clipboard."

"No. According to the girls, he puts his apron on it to let them know not to come in. This is his college dorm! He's actually got them all trained."

Silence. "Are you there now?" he finally asked.

"In the back room? NO! But he is. I want to barge through the door with my phone ready to take pictures." I took another deep breath. My stomach was churning. I fought the urge to kick something. "Please tell me you didn't know this was going on?"

Silence.

"Are you sure?" he asked again.

"The three children he's put in charge of his store told me everything--about the drinks, the lunch--oh, they don't bake blueberry muffins." At this point, I had lost the ability to decipher the bad from the really bad. There's a certain line that when crossed, all evils look the same. "The lead doesn't care for blueberry muffins, so they don't bake them. Where's the Baker anyway? And there's not enough coffee here to last a week." Silence. "Are you there?" I asked.

"Yes," he said. "You're kidding right?"

"That's what I thought when I got here, thought you had set this up. But if this is a joke, you have a very sick mind. There were just three people sitting in the café. It's late morning, and there were only three people sitting in the café! Hello!! Even coffee shops that serve bad coffee have more than that."

"You sure he has someone in the back room?"

"I'm not walking back there. The girls said so, they pointed out the hook on the door displaying his apron. And yes, I heard noises back there. I very much doubt they would make it up if he's back there taking the trash out." Silence. "Maybe that's his cover, he's 'taking the trash out.' You still there?"

"Yes, I'm here. I'm on my way."

"Gregg, you have to bring backup; this is a mess, and it's going to take weeks to get it fixed and months to repair the damage. I think you should call legal, I'm guessing there's a bunch of laws broken here, wouldn't doubt that two of the three behind the counter aren't even sixteen."

"Shit," he said finally. "You're sure?" he asked once again.

"Yes, Gregg, this isn't a joke. I wish it was. Pull up his sales, see the last time they sold a blueberry muffin or what kind of coffee they are selling, he's out of half of them. I'm not joking, I wish I was, but I don't think Suzie could come up with stories like this. I really believe it's happening. If they were so willing to fill me in on the details after they knew who I was, I can't imagine what they've said to customers."

"I'll see you in an hour," he said. "No, wait! I'm packing up now, I'll call you from the car. Don't go back in. Get in your car and get out of sight of the store. I'll call back."

"You're going to have to fix the entire store. We need to replace all the staff. Those that are left have to be really messed up. This sucks, really sucks. How did this happen?"

"I'm sorry," he said. "I'll call you in ten."

Body

The term body describes the physical properties – heaviness, or mouthfeel – of the coffee as it settles on your tongue, the feel of the coffee coating the tongue, and whether it is oily, grainy, watery, or possesses some other characteristic.

Discerning a coffee's body involves identifying its consistency and weight – as perceived in the mouth at the back of the tongue when you swoosh the coffee around in your mouth, and also after swallowing, or after spitting the coffee out if you are a cupper or professional coffee taster.

The coffee's body is a measure of the intensity of how it feels in the mouth in terms of weight, the sense of richness that the brewed coffee imparts, its heft.

12 | Return to Paradise

I pulled out of the parking lot and started driving. I kept imagining bursting into that back room, camera ready, and shouting, "What's up?" The question, *Is he really back there with someone?* rolled over and over in my head. I hadn't spent much time with Kenneth. We had met at the monthly manager meetings. Given the time I had, I wasn't drawn into his *charming* personality. I tried to imagine the type of woman who would be drawn to him and better yet, who would think the back room of a café was a great substitute for a hotel room.

I regard my position as manager with great respect. I think it to be a very important job, one that rarely pays for the level of commitment it requires. I have no tolerance for bad managers. No sympathy for complainers. No pity for gripers. He was setting a precedent that every employee would carry with them the rest of their careers. I had seen my share of bad managers--selfish, insecure, weak, spineless managers--but this was the worst I had ever encountered in my twenty years. This wasn't bad, this was diabolical.

My phone rang, bringing me back to reality.

"Hey," I said.

"Hi. How are you?" Gregg asked.

"Pissed."

"Head back to your store," he instructed.

"With pleasure."

"I'll meet you there."

My heart skipped a beat, and the pit in my stomach was growing into a boulder. "You're not coming here?"

"Not yet." Silence. "You there?" Gregg asked.

"Yes."

"I should be just behind you."

"What are you going to do?" I had a sick feeling he was going to blow this off.

"If it's as bad as you say, we'll need to clean house, and I can't do that this afternoon. I need time. I've called for backup. Someone from Corporate will be visiting the store everyday next week. He'll behave himself if he thinks he has to impress Corporate. He obviously knows how to play the game. I'm not sure how long this has been going on, but the damage is done. Another four or five days can't make it any worse than it already is. In the meantime, I may need you to share some staff."

"Shit, it's them--Gregg, Kenneth's store is calling me--hold on while I take the call. Hello..."

"Hey man, where are you?" It was Kenneth. "The girls said you stopped by but left. I was just out back taking the trash out."

I clenched my jaw. "No...yeah, I was there but my store called... there's a problem with my espresso machine and they're freaking out... got to run back... can't make it without that thing working," I managed to get out.

"You got to toughen those shitheads up," he said. "Tear them down and build them back up the way you want them. They work for you, you don't work for them."

"Spoken like a pro," I said white-knucking the steering wheel.

"You coming back?" he asked.

"I'll see, depends on how long the repairs take. We may need to make it tomorrow." I paused, "Hey, they said you're out of blueberry muffins. Need me to bring you some?"

"Huge rush this morning, someone took a dozen to their office."

"Really, that's great. It looked like your coffee was a little low?"

"Should have been here yesterday, the truck got delayed or something like that."

"That's too bad," I said. I took out my invisible gun and shot the phone.

"Let me know when you're coming back, I'm always here."

"I'll call you this afternoon."

"OK," he said, and he was gone.

"Hello? You still there?" I said.

"Yep. Was that him?"

"Yeah, what an asshole. Told him that my machine is down and have to go back... said I would call him this afternoon to reschedule--maybe tomorrow."

"Wow, I didn't take you for one who could lie so quickly."

"I usually can't! Daniel just said the other day I needed to practice lying. He says I suck at it. So--I have been practicing. Don't know a lot of people who have that on their self-improvement list."

"I don't know anyone," he said. "Now I have another call, see you in an hour," and Gregg hung up.

I drove for a few minutes in silence. The car must have been on auto pilot because I was not paying any attention to where I was going.

"Call Daniel's cell," I eventually said.

"Calling Daniel's cell," said the car's dashboard.

"Hello? Everything all right?" he asked.

"It's been better," I said.

"Thought you were at the other store?"

"I'm heading back already."

"That was fast! How was it?"

"You're not going to believe this."

"No staff?"

"Actually, that would have been a good thing! Apparently, he's servicing women in the back room and has his team covering for him."

"Servicing?"

"Screwing!"

"You're kidding."

"NO. Three idiots behind the counter, cute as can be--of course--all aware of what's going on and didn't seemed bothered at all. Who knows, he's probably doing all of them."

"Sick, so what's happening? They going to fire his sorry ass?"

"Don't know. Gregg's driving to my store, and we're making a plan. I know what's going to happen. They'll tear my team apart to cover over here. I've worked too hard to get my store running well--now this jerk is going to screw it up."

"Don't let them. You don't owe them anything. You didn't hire him."

"I know--but I have a feeling this isn't going to end well."

"Do what you can, but don't put yourself out for this. It's not your store."

"I don't want any of my people over here--yuck, it's disgusting. What kind of bimbo would...I don't even want to think about it."

"Where are you?"

"Still about thirty minutes out."

"Roll down the windows, turn the music up, and try to enjoy the rest of the drive. I love you. It's going to be all right."

"I'll call you when I'm leaving for home. It will be late."

I did as Daniel suggested, rolled down the windows, turned up the music, and tried to wipe the images out of head. Ten minutes later the dashboard rang. I rolled up the windows so I could hear, and the music stopped automatically. "Hey, how's the best Roast Master in the world?" I asked.

"Hi. Everything all right? The other store called and asked if we needed anything while our espresso machine was down."

"What did you say?"

"Well, I glanced over at the machine and watched Becca making drinks. You typically don't lie and the machine was working perfectly so I knew something was up. I reminded myself what store I was talking to--that whole team is crazy. So I said it should only be down for an hour. What's going on?"

"I'm on my way back. The store's a mess--Gregg's coming to our store--we may need to assist in getting it fixed--thanks for covering--glad you're the one who answered."

"How far away are you?"

"You'll see me in 20 minutes."

"OK. Drive safe. You know we'll do anything you ask."

"Thanks, I know... I'm the luckiest girl in the world. I've got the best team ever."

"That isn't luck, sweetie. You work harder than all of us. It'll be okay. See you soon."

"Can't wait to be back in my little home," I said.

Twenty minutes later I stepped through the front doors of paradise. I stopped and listened to the conversation and the laughter. There was guitar music coming from the patio, a fresh batch of cinnamon rolls had just emerged from the oven filling the store with comfort. The espresso machine was humming as Becca was frothing milk with six cups lined up in front of her, all the while carrying on a conversation with a customer waiting for his drink. Suzie stood behind the counter and burst into laughter as a customer delivered the punch line of a joke. I looked over the bakery case, assuring that the blueberry muffins were in their place of honor. Upon seeing them, a sense of relief rushed through me... as if the world pivoted on their existence.

"This is how it's supposed to be. This is why I do this," I said to myself. I walked into the back room and was greeted by my Roaster, Baker, and Magic Maker. I looked at the three of them and realized my appreciation for all of them had just skyrocketed.

"Welcome back boss," Barry the Baker said. Barry was an ex-basketball player. He stood 6 foot 5 inches tall. I remember watching him duck through the door on the day I interviewed him. He had been a star player in high school, a mediocre player in college, and after getting his business degree, decided he wanted to be a baker. Barry worked a few odd jobs in the bakeries of local grocery stores before applying at Inkwell. I fell in love with him the moment we shook hands.

"So, it's really a mess?" Renee the Roaster asked. Renee was no-nonsense, as black and white as they come.

"A real mess," I said.

"Doesn't surprise me," Barry said.

"Really?" I asked.

"We were just talking about it and realized that all our counterparts from Kenneth's store called us before they quit. The three of us just never put it all together," Barry said.

"I heard rumblings but was so focused on getting us up and running, I just let it go."

"Well, it's not your store," Renee said.

"I know, but it's our company. More than that, I hurt for the people that work or worked for him."

"Before his baker quit, I got a call from her. She was frustrated but said she was too old for a battle. She knew it would get ugly. She asked if I was planning on leaving anytime soon, she wanted to come here."

"So--how bad is it?" Renee asked.

I hesitated. The three stood looking at me.

I closed my eyes, "He's screwing customers in the back room." Silence...then laughter.

"No fucking way," Barry said and immediately covered his mouth. "I'm sorry," he said.

"No need, been saying it all the way home."

I watched as each one tried to comprehend the disastrous situation. All three looked around our back room. They started to form a word but no sound would come out, then they scanned the back room again.

"Yep. Apparently, he even has a system. From the condition of the store, it's the only system he has." They were still struggling to form words. "Gregg's on his way over. I know he's going to ask if we can help. I don't want to screw us because... well, because he's screwing." For the first time, I began to see the humor of the situation. "You can also get free lunches. They're exchanging free drinks for free food."

"Seriously?" Barry asked.

"How do you know all this?" inquired Renee.

"They either told me or told each other while I was standing there. Imagine what they've told customers."

"What a mess." We stood in our little circle trying to make sense of it.

"We'll do whatever it takes," Renee said.

"I know you will. We'll see what Gregg has planned." I shrugged my shoulders and realized that I was smiling.

"I think they would come back," Barry said.

"Who would?"

"The team, or at least this group," Barry pointed at his co-workers. "They were good. We all went through training together. I really think if they thought it was fixable, they would go back."

"If they were good, and I trust your judgment, that would be amazing," I said.

"Bring them here for a week, let them see how it should work."

"Would you be willing to do that?" I asked. "That's a lot of extra work."

"Of course," Stephanie said. It was the first she had spoken up. Stephanie stood two inches taller than me, she had been a model, and we could all see why--she was drop dead gorgeous. She had left modeling when she married. She and her soon-to-be-doctor husband had moved to the area when he accepted a position at the hospital. She had blond hair, blue eyes, and her German accent was still very prevalent. She was our Magic Maker, and she was one of the best.

"I greatly appreciate that," I said. "Right now, I just want us all to go on playing store and forget the whole thing."

The back door flung open. "Important meeting?"

"Hello, Sir," Barry said as he saluted Gregg.

"Is there a reason why the blue light it flashing?" he asked. We all froze. He started laughing. "Just kidding." We all exhaled in relief.

We four just stood there looking at Gregg.

"You told them?" he asked. I nodded. "I thought I had seen it all." Renee rolled her eyes, Stephanie shivered, and Barry snickered.

"Barry thinks you could get his main team back. They're suggesting that we bring them here for a week before we send them back over there. It's worth a few calls," I said.

"You really think so?" Gregg said addressing Barry directly. He nodded.

"They are good people and think it's worth contacting them to try to get them back."

"Well, that's good news. Grab your schedule and let's go get a table. We've got work to do."

"You've got work to do," I said.

Gregg smiled. "Yes, I do, and I need your help."

"Say that again, please...just the part about needing my help."

"No, I'll only say that once."

"As long as you remember that these next four weeks--you need me!"

"In your dreams," he replied.

"This is more like a nightmare, and I would gladly wake up anytime," I said.

"Party in the back room?" Suzie asked, as she flung the door open, slamming it against the wall.

"Renee," I said. "Please remember to put a door stopper on the next supply order. We're going to be able to see right into the dressing rooms soon."

"Back to work! Chop, chop. There are drinks to be made, beans to be roasted, and big guy," Suzie said addressing Barry, "I need more chocolate chip cookies, just sold six of them."

Gregg turned around, "Suzie, how would you feel about helping out at another store for a bit?"

"In your dreams!" I said. "She's not going anywhere!"

"We'll see..."

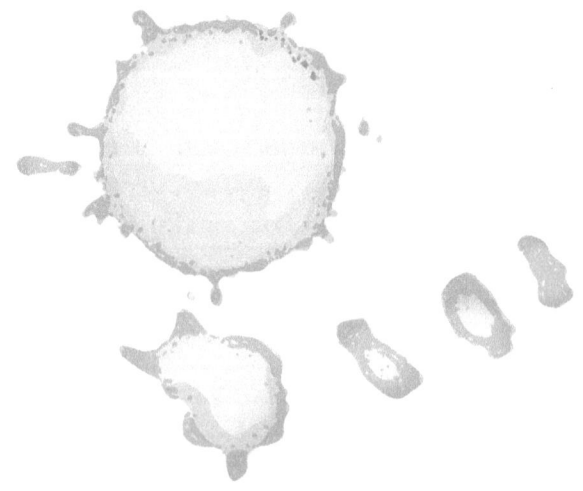

Espresso

Espresso is a strong black coffee made by forcing steam through dark-roast aromatic coffee beans at high pressure. A perfectly brewed espresso will have a thick, golden-brown crema (foam) on the surface. If the crema is good, the sugar you add will float on the surface for a couple of seconds before slowly sinking to the bottom.

Espresso is the foundation for a wide variety of specialty coffee drinks, such as cappuccino and latte.

"Short" means that it has less water and is therefore more concentrated.

"Long" conversely uses more water and does not taste as strong.

Adding a dollop of steamed milk creates an espresso macchiato ("macchiato" means stained or marked).

Topping an espresso with whipped cream is called espresso con panna.

13 | The End of Summer

Kenneth, the manager from hell, was fired. It seemed to take him and his entire staff by surprise proving the saying, *incompetent people don't know they are incompetent.*

Taking the trash out was not the only issue in the back room. A gallon glass jar sat just above the desk, filled to the top with coins. When I inquired about its existence and purpose, the response was simple, "Cause we can't deposit coins at the bank, they don't accept them. So we put all the coins in there."

"What do you mean, we can't deposit coins?" I asked.

"Ken says the bank doesn't allow it so we put the coins in there, and he takes care of it," the team leader said with great confidence.

I just stared at him. *A bank that doesn't take coins? Really? Where did he find these people?* "How often do you think he changes it out?" I asked.

"It's full by the end of the week," the employee said.

"Every week?" I asked.

"Sure. Ken dumps it into a plastic bag and takes it home. He says it's company policy."

"Have you ever seen it in writing?" I asked.

"No. But I'm sure it's in the Manager's Training Guide."

Needless to say, most of the team who had been there when Kenneth was let go also left. Those that remained only lasted a few weeks, as they quickly realized that they were going to be expected to follow a few rules. I'm certain the realization that there was no longer a free flow of food coming into the front door in exchange for free drinks also weighed in. We had not only fired their boss, we had cut off their food chain.

My team rose to the challenge and did as they promised. Our store became the training store. Some days we were tripping over staff, there were so many of us. Fortunately, there was an Assistant Manager from another location who was waiting for a position to open. When Kenneth's position opened, she jumped at the chance. It was a great relief, as I only needed to assist her in transitioning.

It was a very different scenario than having to run two stores. I was in my store three days a week and at the troubled store the other three. I somehow managed to keep one day off. Besides wanting to see the store fixed, I had sold myself on the idea that the reimbursed mileage for those six weeks would make a nice vacation fund. Of course, there was no time for a vacation, but when there was, it would be funded.

Barry was right, the Roaster and Baker returned after they were assured Kenneth was gone. The original Magic Maker from Kenneth's store had the wind blown out of her sails and wanted nothing to do with the store or company. Stephanie stepped in and split her time between the two stores. She had become well connected in the art community and used those connections to build relationships in our sister store. She was making magic in both locations.

Fall was coming and I felt as if I had missed the entire summer. I hadn't agreed to take on the failing store immediately. When I finally said "yes," it was partly because I knew I could do it, but mostly because I figured if I went in and did it right, I would not have to deal with them ever again. It was a risk to be dividing my time between two stores simply because we were still in our first year. But with the support of my Roaster, Baker, and Magic Maker, we could attack it as a team, and they would benefit from the experience.

Suzie instinctively took control of our store and kept it running when I was gone. She was the constant one as we all ran around like crazy people, a complete reversal. Usually she was the crazy one, and we were the constant.

"Why aren't you a manager?" I asked one day, as I began brewing green tea and Suzie was measuring out ground coffee for the next day.

"Cause that's your job," she replied.

"I know, but you could be one."

"Nope," she said very confidently. "Don't want to be one; I love interacting with people, I love coming to work and working my ass off. But what I really love, is walking out that door and taking nothing with me."

"Someday," I said.

"Not hardly," she said.

"I suppose. We've got to get you on that espresso machine first."

"That can wait."

"You're going to have to do it," I said. "You can't be on the registers all your life."

She gave me a look that made it clear: we had waited this long without an issue, and she intended to keep it that way.

"Hey, is the invisible man still coming, haven't seen him lately," I said, changing the subject so as not to ruffle the diva's feathers.

"He's been here, you just haven't noticed."

"Oh yeah, that's right... Got any closer to knowing what he does?"

"No. But I have a plan. I'm breaking him down."

"I'm sure you are."

My time at the other store grew less frequent and I was thrilled. We had new customers at my store that I needed to meet. I had become the stranger. When my responsibilities were finally finished at the second store, I drove back to my café, rolled down the windows, turned up the music, and let all the memories and images of the past six weeks fly away. The only image that remained was the black apron hung on the door, that would be burned in my head forever.

As I pulled into the parking lot I loved, I saw red lights flashing.

"Wow, we almost made it ninety days without overheating, must be a record." I parked and got out. As I walked toward the front door, I noticed people standing on the patio and lined up on the sidewalk. "This isn't the beans," I said, as I picked up my pace.

As I reached the sidewalk, Barry came around the corner with a tray of cookies and was passing them out to customers. I made my way over to him, "What's happening?" I asked.

"Hey, boss, welcome back!"

"Thanks, but what's happening?"

"Oh, this? They think it's an electrical fire."

"In the roaster?"

"No, the women's bathroom. They suspect a faulty ceiling fan."

I recognized the fire chief and walked over to him. "Hey, I'm Jenn. I'm the store manager. Can you fill me in?"

"Hi," he said reaching out his hand. "Suzie said you were on your way."

"She's still here?" I asked looking at my watch and then into the store.

"Does Suzie ever leave?" the fire chief asked. "She's taken great care of us. I may have a difficult time getting the men back to the station." We both chuckled. "Anyway, looks like an electrical fire started in the women's bathroom, the ceiling fan I suspect. It's been disconnected, the danger is over, but I wouldn't let anyone in until it can air out and the room can be cleaned up. Health Department will need to be contacted, they have to do a safety check. I'm guessing they'll just say to tape off the restroom."

"That bad?" I asked.

"You'll be surprised. These things happen so quickly. I'm guessing it's because you have so much fresh air flowing through the store that no one really noticed the fumes. The bath room is going to have to be gutted."

"Gutted? It's not even a year old. It's that bad?" I asked again hoping for a different answer.

"It got pretty hot in there, lots of melted plastic, that's the worst of it."

"Here you go," Suzie had ducked under the yellow tape and was handing the fire chief a large latte. "Hey Boss, welcome home!" she said.

"You're still here?"

"Well, you know, men in uniform and all... just couldn't pull myself away. The big guy had just pulled tonight's bakery out of the oven so he's walking around handing it out. We're brewing coffee, thought we could set up on the patio and give it away."

"Would that be all right?" I asked the chief.

"I don't see why not. I would stay clear of serving from the bar 'till the health inspector arrives, but I don't think they'll have an issue with coffee." He took a sip of his latte, "You're the best," he said as he toasted Suzie.

Suzie took a bow. "Hey, big guy," she called over to Barry, "got any left?", excusing herself and walked toward him.

"That's a keeper," the chief said.

"I pray every day that she doesn't leave me."

"Just a reminder to keep the patio doors open; you'll have to keep someone posted so customers don't walk in. The health inspector will tell you what else you need to do."

"Thanks," I said reaching out to shake his hand again. I ducked under the yellow tape and through the front doors. The smell of cinnamon and coffee had been replaced with the stench of burning plastic. Except for the unusual odor and the obvious disappearance of customers, nothing seemed damaged. I walked down the short hall to the restrooms. The women's door was propped open. "Holy shit," I said gazing into a black hole.

"Bad, isn't it," Renee said from behind me. "At least it wasn't me or the roaster."

"Really bad. Who would have thought? Look, the toilet seat melted," I said.

"It could have been much worse."

"Who found it?" I asked.

"We heard a scream from the hall, and the barista came running over from the bar. A customer had opened the door and a wall of smoke billowed out. The smell was awful. Barry and I started escorting customers out through the patio, and Becca called 911. Suzie had just clocked out and was in her car when she heard the sirens. She followed the firemen in. She got coffee brewing to serve on the patio."

"Has anyone called Gregg?"

"Don't think so." Renee put her hand on my shoulder, "I don't even know if we called you?" We both laughed.

"Thanks," I said, "I feel so needed."

"Hey, Boss," Barry shouted as he ducked through the front doors. The rest of us were bending down to fit under the yellow tape, he was ducking under the door frame and stepped over the tape. "Want a cookie?"

"Sure, why not," I said. "It will give me energy to call the big boss."

Barry walked over with his tray of cookies... "It's bad, isn't it? They're going to have to gut it."

"That's what the chief thought."

I heard the phone ring in the distance. Becca answered, "Hey Gregg! How's your day?--Yes, we're having a great day--She just got back, she's right here." Becca walked over and handed me the phone.

I covered the mouthpiece, "You didn't think you should tell him?" Becca shrugged her shoulders as if it was just another day at the Inkwell. I took the phone and walked toward the back room. "Hey," I said.

"How's your day going?" he asked.

"Interesting," I said. "Just got back from the other store, they'er doing all right. A few more weeks and they should be back to where they started."

"I'm heading over tomorrow and plan to spend the rest of the week there."

"That will be good. Just don't mess them up too much," I said. "We've worked hard to get them to do it right." He laughed. "For Pete's sake, don't get on the bar or registers, stick to washing dishes."

"Very funny," he said. "Anything else?"

"You don't know?" I asked.

"Know what?"

"Well, my store is vacant of customers, filled with the stench of burnt plastic, there's two fire trucks, an ambulance, a police car, and rescue unit in my parking lot."

"The roaster?"

"No, the fan in the women's bathroom shorted out and created so much heat it melted the fixtures. The health inspector is on his way to access, so we have to wait for his approval before we let people back in. They say the restroom has to be gutted."

"You're kidding, right?"

"No, I'm dead serious. I've been here a whole fifteen minutes. It all happened while I was driving back."

"Why didn't they call me?"

"They didn't even call me!" I said. "I drove up and saw the lights."

"Are we giving coffee away?" He asked.

"Suzie's all over it. Barry's handing out free bakery, and Suzie's setting up brewed coffee on the patio. We can't let anyone in."

"You're kidding, right?" He asked again.

"No Gregg, I'll send you a picture. The women's bathroom is a black hole, the store stinks, and there are five firefighters talking to Suzie on the patio. Good thing they didn't call you--you wouldn't have believed them!" We both laughed. "So, what do I do now?"

"I guess you wait for the health inspector. I'll be there first thing in the morning, or should I come over tonight?"

"There's nothing you can do until the health inspector gets here, and I doubt that will be soon. Don't make a special trip. If we're still not operational in the morning, we'll set up on the front sidewalk and give it away. I'll ask the inspector if we can bake; if we can, we'll give out samples."

"Anything else you need?"

"What, you mean with everything else you've done for us today?"

Gregg laughed and once again I was grateful he got my humor. "Well, I do my best," he said.

"Order us pizza, it's going to be a long night."

"Done!" he said.

"Thanks," I said. "I'd better go. I'll call you after I talk with the inspector." I laid the phone on the counter and made my way through the store.

"Was that the inspector?" Suzie asked as I walked onto the patio.

"No, Gregg. He's ordering us pizza."

"Nice," she said.

"How long are you hanging around?" I asked. "Don't you turn into a pumpkin soon?"

"Eight o'clock," she said. "I'm useless after 8:00 p.m."

"I'll keep that in mind. Did you clock back in?"

She paused and looked up trying to recall. "No, don't think I did."

"Are we volunteering tonight?"

"Hardly," she said. "You'll fix it, right?"

"Yes, I'll fix it...that's what I do."

On this beautiful summer evening, Suzie and I stood side by side handing out free coffee on the patio that faced the ocean. We repeated the story of the wall of smoke and the horrific smell, the fire trucks, and that we were waiting for the inspector. We ate our pizza and invited the pizza delivery guy to join us. Baker Barry stuffed us with an evening's worth of sugar.

It wasn't until the sun was setting that I made it home. I had fulfilled my obligations at the other store and as of this afternoon, I became the manager of one location. Even covered with a thin layer of soot and filled with a nasty stench, it was home and I loved it.

THE BASICS

Cappuccino
A true cappuccino is a combination of equal parts espresso, steamed milk and milk froth. This luxurious drink, if made properly, can double as a dessert with its complex flavors and richness.

Caffe Latte
A caffe latte is a single shot of espresso to three parts of steamed milk.

Caffe au Lait
This traditional French drink is similar to a caffe latte except that it is made with brewed coffee instead of espresso, in a 1:1 ratio with steamed milk. It is considered a weaker form of caffe latte.

Caffe Mocha (Mochachino)
This is a cappuccino or a caffe latte with chocolate syrup or powder and garnished with whipped cream.

14 | Signs
Do Not Enter

The sun blinded me as I walked out onto the café patio for my weekly meeting with the Roaster, the Baker, and the Magic Maker. I wondered if I would ever refer to them by their given names. It had been a week since the fire. We had only been closed until noon the following day, when the health inspector gave the all clear.

There were large orange signs lining the restroom hallway. Some reading DO NOT ENTER and others informing our guests that we now only had one working restroom, and it would be unisex until repairs of the women's was complete.

I sat down at our usual table, the others already in their seats. "What's your response when you see a DO NOT ENTER sign?" I asked.

"Nothing," Stephanie, the Magic Maker said.

"Nothing, like you don't enter or nothing, like you don't obey it?" I asked.

"Nothing, like I don't enter. Someone put it there for a reason, and it's not for me to ask why," she said.

"Barry, what do you do?"

Barry thought for a moment, "I guess such a sign would make me curious. I would want to open the door to see why I wasn't supposed to open the door."

"And Renee, what's your reaction?"

She began laughing. "Usually, I don't even see the sign or I figure it doesn't pertain to me. What do you do?" she asked.

"I'm more like Barry. It makes me want to open the door and find out why I'm not supposed to be opening the door."

"Can we make some room here?" Suzie asked, now standing next to the table with a tray of small white tasting cups, three French presses, and a few small bowls in her hands. We all grabbed our notebooks and papers that were spread across the table. "Renee's done it again! She has chosen three very different coffees for your tasting today. I'm really excited about this one!" Suzie set the tray down and sat down next to me.

"Suzie, what do you do when you see a DO NOT ENTER sign?" I asked.

"I don't enter," she said very matter-of-fact.

"Really? That surprises me," I said.

"I like rules," she said with a childish smile. "I like following rules."

"This, too, surprises me," I said. I attempted to avoid the slap on the shoulder I was sure was coming, but she got me. I rubbed the wound for effect. "Careful, that seat is for guests of honor; I can take the honor away."

"Threats, threats," she said settling into her chair.

I shook my head and rolled my eyes, a typical response to Suzie. "Take it away, Renee," I said.

"We've got to do a better job of describing our coffees," she began. "The other day I heard a customer ask about Sumatra and the response was, 'It's good.'"

"It's good?" I interrupted. "Of course it's good, who said that?"

"Doesn't matter," Renee said. "We're going to fix it. We've got to take the time to increase everyone's coffee knowledge. I've mapped out the next eight weeks that will allow us to focus on three different coffees each week. By the end of the cycle, everyone should be able to describe, compare, and taste the differences in the coffees," Renee explained as she handed out the coffee tasting calendar.

"I don't see any coffee described as 'good'. You think we can handle this?" I said.

She continued ignoring me, "We're going to start with basics. The three main growing regions: South America, Africa, and Indonesia."

Suzie set out the five small white handleless cups, poured from the first French press and gave us each one.

"We're going to start with the three growing regions, then each week we'll build on a region. For this first week, it's a very broad view." Renee took one of the three bowls from the tray--in it was a cut lemon and small flower petals. She laid one of each next to each cup. "The first coffee is South America, we have Costa Rica today. South American coffees are usually described as clean and bright with hints of citrus and floral notes. Let's begin by smelling the coffee." We did as we were instructed. "As you are smelling, look down at the lemon and flower petal."

"Oh my," Barry said. "It makes those flavors come alive!"

Among the "mmms" and "ahhs," Stephanie quietly admitted, "I'm not getting it."

"Pick up the flower and smell it." Steph followed Renee's instructions. "Now the lemon." Again Steph did as instructed. "Now, hold that little cup in your hands and breathe in deeply."

Stephanie did as she was instructed. I watched with great anticipation. "Keep doing it," Renee encouraged.

Around the fourth sniff of lemon and then coffee, Stephanie lit up, "I smell it!" She said. "I really smell it! I've never done that before." We all applauded her great achievement.

"OK, now sip. Remember to get a lot of air in your mouth as you taste--if you're not slurping, you're not doing it right."

We all began making slurping noises, which made us laugh so hard that we almost spit out the coffee. Renee waited patiently. "Everyone over the giggles?" she finally asked. "Do it again." We did. "Let the coffee roll around on your tongue. Do you get it? Are you tasting the citrus?" We all nodded. "Great!" she said.

I glanced over at Stephanie who was lost in her little world of flavor and aroma. Tasting and smelling the nuances of coffee for the first time is magical.

Suzie set up another round and poured from the second French press. Renee took the white bowl containing blueberries and blackberries and set a few in front of each of us. She then reached under her chair and retrieved a bottle of red wine.

"I don't think we have a license for that!" I said.

"It's empty, don't worry," she replied. "The second growing region is Africa. These coffees are typically described as medium bodied with berry and winey notes. Let's smell first." We each brought our cups to our noses and inhaled. "Look at the berries and wine bottle as you do so, these are the flavors you're looking for--Steph, you getting it?"

Stephanie's eyes were closed as she breathed in the aroma. "She's getting it," I said.

"All right, slurp--no laughing this time." The table slurped in unison as the dark, rich, syrupy goodness filled our mouths. As we allowed the coffee to roll around on our tongues, the flavor of berries and wine brushed across our taste buds. "Got it?" We all nodded.

"Now, I want you to take a sip of the Costa Rica, go on, quickly. Just a sip." We did as instructed.

"Holy Cow!" Suzie rang out. "What a difference." Renee sat nodding her head, very satisfied with the reaction.

"Now for the last tasting, Suzie if you please." Suzie filled the last five cups from the third press, and Renee pulled a small brown bag from under her chair. She reached in and retrieved what looked like small cubes of sod. Upon closer inspection, that is just what it was. She placed a sod cube in front of each of us and set a dark piece of chocolate on top.

"We're comparing this to chocolate grass?" I asked.

"Not sure if that's good or bad," Barry offered.

"Depends on what kind of grass we are speaking about," Suzie quipped.

"Can we graduate from junior high already?" Renee said shaking her head in disapproval. "Our final region is Indonesia. Sumatra is described as a full bodied coffee; it is earthy, syrupy with chocolate overtones. Let's smell."

"Wow, this is distinct," Barry said.

"Before you taste it, let's compare its aroma to the Costa Rican." We picked up the first cup and breathed in its aroma then did the same with the Sumatra.

"Like night and day," I said.

"Exactly. South Americans are bright and light--great breakfast coffees; where Sumatra is bold and rich--great for deserts, evening. All right, go ahead and slurp, don't forget to look at our taste samples."

Five of us slurped like pros. As the coffee swirled around on our tongues, we couldn't help but smile.

"It's amazing! Seeing the image makes the flavors come alive," Barry said.

"Coffee should excite our senses. By seeing the flavors, it heightens our taste and smell. Three of the five senses working together."

"I've always thought that touch should be included in that. There's something about wrapping your hands around the cup and bringing it to your mouth. We may not be touching the actual coffee, but that cup is a vital part."

"It's the whole experience."

We sat for a few more moments, each revisiting their favorite, each allowing the flavors and aromas to take us to faraway places. "Renee, thanks for this, very well done."

"When do we start doing it with the team?"

"I've got the schedule and have found times when I can pull two or three aside for a tasting. Again, we'll start with the broad view then dial it in a little," Renee said.

"Can we offer this for our customers?" Stephanie asked.

"Of course!" I said without hesitation. "What are you thinking?"

"I'd love to set up some half-hour tastings these next eight weeks. We should share our knowledge," she said.

"Set it up! If Renee isn't available to lead them, I'd be happy to," I said.

Suzie began clearing the table. She stood, but quickly sat right back down again. "Little light headed?" I asked. She nodded.

"Between the smelling, the slurping, and the caffeine, it can create a little buzz."

"It's called being Caffeinated!" Barry said.

"Thanks for the heads up," Suzie said resting her head in her hands.

"Barry, can you grab some bread, either a croissant or muffin? Suzie needs something to strengthen her coffee legs. Don't worry dear, you'll get used to it."

She looked at Renee, "This doesn't bother you?" she asked.

"It's a way of life. I live caffeinated!"

"Did you miss that in training?" I asked. "The part that says we make a living selling a legal drug that we hope everyone gets hooked on and keeps coming back?"

"I think I missed that," she smiled.

"Hang out as long as you need, it will pass shortly," I said. Suzie sat with us for a few minutes. When she had regained her sea legs, she slowly finished clearing the table and walked into the back room. I had never seen her walk so slowly. My Roaster, Baker, and Magic Maker spent another hour together going over the next week's schedule and looking ahead at the fall calendar.

At 3:00 p.m., I took over the bar and played barista. I loved working the bar; I challenged myself every time I was on it to go a little faster. I never wanted to be the old manager who made everyone nervous when I was working bar. I somehow felt that if I could keep up with the best, I wouldn't seem so old.

We had a busier than normal afternoon and I was hopping. Barry had pulled the evening fare from the ovens, and the store smelled heavenly. Both Stephanie and Barry stepped behind the counter several times to assist with the line. Bob came in at his expected time; it never mattered to Bob how busy we were, he parked himself at the end of the bar and dialogued with anyone who would listen. When there was no one listening, he just kept on talking 'till there was someone.

As Bob stood at the end of the counter watching and slipping in a few comments from time to time, a woman in her mid-fifties with dark black hair styled as if she lived in the 1970's, walked up to the bar. "Are you the manager?" she asked.

I had to lean over to hear her. "I'm sorry, what did you say?"

"Are you the manager?" she said leaning closer but not talking any louder. I nodded. "I just wanted to let you know that the restrooms need cleaning."

"Oh, thank you so much. We've been a little crazy, and I'm sure it was overlooked." I looked over at the screen and saw four more orders pop up. I looked back at her and for some unknown reason said, "Thanks again for letting me know. You are talking about the men's restroom, correct?"

"No," she shook her head, "the women's."

Bob had just taken a swig of coffee and did everything he could to not spew it out again. He looked up at me, I didn't dare look at him. I swallowed, bit my lips. "You used the women's restroom?"

She nodded with the innocence of a child. "I'm so sorry, we had a fire in that one a week ago and it isn't to be used. I'm sorry you didn't see the signs."

"Oh," she replied and walked away, completely unaffected.

Bob glared up at me, "did I just hear that right?"

"I think we did," I said. Two more orders popped up on the screen.

"Jenn, do you need any help over there?" Becca called from the register.

"Yeah, can you cover for a minute?"

Becca replaced me at the bar. "What's going on?" I heard her ask Bob as I walked down the hallway.

"You'll never believe it," was all he said.

I looked at the five orange signs that lined the hallway, most of them taped at eye level. I first opened the door to the men's room to examine it. It was clean, used, but clean. I then opened the women's door; the room was still covered in black soot, the toilet seat all melted, disfigured, and barely hanging on to its hinges. I stepped in and closed the door. The room went pitch black, I couldn't see my hand in front of my face. The knock on the door scared the crap out of me.

"You all right in there?" Barry asked.

I opened the door. He started laughing. "I've never seen that expression," he said.

"You'll never believe it," I said. "We just had the--I don't even know how to describe her--most bizzare customer on the face of the planet." I told him the story and as the words "no, the women's" left my lips, Barry put his head back and bellowed. We stood there laughing until tears ran down our cheeks.

It went on for minutes. We couldn't stop. I grabbed his arm to balance myself. When we finally gained a morsel of composure, we walked back into the café only to find Bob bent over wheezing in laughter. Becca was trying to call out drinks, but she was shaking so hard she could barely hold the cups. Renee had stepped behind the registers and was apologizing for the insanity. She said we had all overdosed on caffeine and that it was a job hazard.

The more we tried to gain control, the more we lost it. I glanced around the café hoping not to see the bathroom lady, and to my great relief, she wasn't to be found. What I did see was a café full of customers grinning from ear to ear. Some were even chuckling behind book pages. Our laughter was contagious.

Ristretto Shot

A Ristretto shot is a short shot of espresso which means that the brewing time is shortened although the amount of water used is the same.

By allowing the hot water to have a shorter contact time than normal with the roasted and ground coffee, the goal is to extract less of the caffeine relative to the flavorful coffee oils. The classic Ristretto shot emphasizes body and sweetness.

The body of a Ristretto shot is fuller and bolder than a normal shot, while at the same time being less bitter. The flavor of a Ristretto shot is said to be exaggerated compared to a typical espresso shot.

15 | Dented Refrigerators

September arrived in all its west coast beauty. In our little world, fall was the best time of the year--blue skies, warm temperatures, and ocean breezes. As predictable as the season changes, so are the staff changes that happen in fall; students leaving, new ones arriving. For those of us who attended traditional schools as kids, we have an instilled internal clock that says, summer is for playing, fall is for starting new things.

Jackie was a new thing. She was entering the masters program at the university in town in the field of psychology. When I interviewed her she seemed pleasant and responsible, a no-nonsense kind of girl. I assumed she might be able to help us or if nothing else use us as a case study. She might be able to assist Suzie in breaking the code of the invisible man. Or help us understand Suzie. I thought she was a perfect fit.

The invisible man continued to visit the café. He never missed a day and never gave more than a two word answer. With the beginning of a new season, Suzie had a new strategy to get him to speak more than two words. Each morning, she would greet the invisible man with a new imagined name and ask how his day was going. She would then ask how he liked being an accountant, or dectective, or banker. Each day was a new career and each day was a new ficticious name. The downfall of this strategy was that she had to get the combination correct--name and career--because all the invisible man would give her was a single answer, "no." She tried to correct the problem with clarification, but he would have nothing to do with it; he only shook his head and walked away.

I was watching him one particular morning as he sat reading the paper. It was a perfect morning, and the rhythm of the store was dead on. There is an amazing energy that ignites when the team is on their game. There is chatter and laughter, joking and storytelling.

Suzie had some of the best stories ever of the two aunts she had lived with as a child. These two elderly ladies stilled lived in the same little house they did when Suzie was a kid. She told us of her trips going to visit and sleeping up in her old room. The years had decayed the place and she could see the sky through the ceiling rafters. They loved their world and no one wanted to take them from it. Suzie told of departed family members whose remains were safely tucked away in containers under the furniture.

There was always an absurd news article that kept us and our customers engaged. When the rhythm is right, everyone gets caught up in the music. The fact that we were all buzzed on caffeine never hurt. This particular morning my new hire, Jackie was backing me up on the bar.

The invisible man's table was in direct view as I stood behind the bar. He sat down, opened his paper, and began to read. I glanced over just as Suzie burst into laughter at the punch line of a joke. I watched as he ever so slightly repositioned his paper to get a look at what was happening. It was not enough to appear interested, just enough to observe.

"He's engaged!" I said softly.

"Whose engaged?" Jackie asked.

"The invisible man, watch..."

"Jackie, can you get me an extra large iced coffee?" Suzie asked.

"Sure," she said. I watched as Jackie reached for a hot cup, filled it with ice, and began to pour coffee over it. To my delight, she stopped after the first few drops of the hot coffee poured over the ice. "This isn't right, is it?"

I shook my head. "Cold press," I said, half telling and half asking.

"The Devil's Cup," Suzie said in her sinister voice.

"That's right," Jackie said, suddenly remembering her training. "Cold press, that's in this refrigerator, right?"

I nodded. She reached down and retrieved a gallon pitcher filled with dark, rich coffee syrup. There was always a batch of cold press being made. One pound of coffee would be placed into a half-gallon plastic container then covered with water. The brew would sit for twenty-four hours and then be drained.

"That's liquid gold, Texas Tea!" I said.

"That can do damage," Suzie warned. "It's the Devils Cup!"

"NO!" Becca burst out, taking Jackie by surprise. Upon further inspection, she was just responding to the ending of her customer's tales of the weekend!

The invisible man was watching every interaction from his front row seat. *He's not invisible, we're just his morning entertainment,* I thought.

"What are you doing over there?" Suzie asked, pounding her fist on the counter.

I ducked down behind the espresso machine and held my finger up to my lips to shush her, "Spying!" I whispered.

Suzie looked at me with great delight, she could never resist a spy story. She then looked back at her next customer, held up her index finger and said, "I'll be right back, very important discovery." Crouching down, she crept over to the bar. *I watched as her customer observed; by Suzie's third step, he began to laugh. By the next step, she had Becca and her customer's full attention as well.

Suzie crept closer, she knew how to work a crowd. I bit my lip to keep from laughing. She had her hands over her mouth and her head ducked low. As she got closer, I held up my index finger to those waiting for their drinks and said, "I'll be right back," and pointed down to where Suzie was slumped over, "crazy employee," I said, and then I joined her, both of us crouched down behind the bar.

"Suzie," I whispered, "the invisible man is watching everything we do." She shot up, looked over at him, and crouched right back down. I began to wheeze-laugh like the cartoon dog Muttley, Dick Dastardly's sidekick. Suzie remained crouched over as she shuffled back to her register.

She straightened up, smiled, and asked her patiently waiting guest, "Whatcha having?" as if nothing had happened. I snuck a peek at the invisible man; he was still pretending to be reading his paper but he was smiling.

"Just another day in the loony bin," I said to the customer waiting for his beverage.

As we were finishing our shift and the next crew was exiting from the back room, Jackie inquired, "What time will our paychecks be here?"

"FedEx is usually here by 3:00 p.m.," I said. "This is your first check, right?"

"Yeah, I really need it."

"Do you want me to call you when they get here?" I asked.

"No, I'll just stop by," she replied.

"You better give it 'till four, he can vary sometimes."

I sat at my desk writing schedules after the lunch rush was over, so deep in thought and lost in a manager's altered universe that I didn't hear her come in. It took some time before I realized there was the dark shadow of a person standing next to me. Glancing down at their feet, I knew by the leather steel-toe boots tucked neatly under the cuffed black jeans that it was Renee. She could never find pants short enough.

"Can I help you?" I asked not looking around. I waited but there was silence. Turning, I looked up with raised brow. Renee was unsuccessfully attempting to form words. "What is it?" I encouraged. "You can tell me."

"There's a rat in the store."

"You mean in the beans?" She shook her head. "Did it come in through the patio?" She shook her head again. "You're going to have to give me more than just the facts on this one." She blankly stared at me. "Have the customers seen it?" She nodded. "Renee, what the hell is going on?"

At that moment, the back door flung open and Barry ducked in. "Hey boss, some chick out here has a rat running up and down her arms."

"What!"

"Yeah, she's letting a rat run up one arm, across her shoulders, and down the other. I saw it dance a little jig on her head during one crossing."

"She came in with it?" Renee nodded. "She can't bring a rat into the store!" Renee shook her head. I scooted my chair back. "I've got to see this," I said walking toward the door and motioning Renee to follow.

The three of us exited the back room together, caught the attention of the barista who calmly asked, "Here to see the rat lady?"

Barry pointed and I stood in disbelief as I watched a skinny, long-haired woman in her early twenties sit calmly as a creature smaller than a rat but larger than a mouse crawled up one arm, across her shoulders and back down the other. On its return trip, it crawled up her hair and ran in circles atop her head. I shivered. Barry huffed, and Renee leaned into me. "She can't bring that in here," she whispered.

I looked back at her, "Ya think?"

I looked up at Barry, as he stood tall shaking his head. "It's weird, I wonder if she needs a permit for that? Maybe it's her service pet."

"That's one service pet that can't run free, not in a restaurant, not in my store!"

Barry patted me on the shoulder, "Go get um' boss."

"Thanks. I'll take care of her," I said thumbing back in Renee's direction.

"Gotcha," he said.

I walked toward the table, grateful that no one was sitting in the seat behind her. Imagine sitting in a café, drinking your favorite beverage and have a rat jump on your shoulder and dance a jig on your head. I shivered again. Just as I reached the table, a young man breezed by me and took the seat across from the rat lady. *Really?* I thought. *She has a boyfriend?*

I stepped up to the table. "Good afternoon," I said with a forced smile. "That's an interesting pet."

The rat lady smiled so large that it wrinkled her nose and made her eyes squint. She really liked this thing. "How do you carry him?" I inquired.

"He rides in my backpack," she said in a soft sweet voice. It was such a soft sweet female voice that if she wasn't sitting in front of me I would have thought she was a young child.

"Do you take him in restaurants with you?" I said, trying to sound intrigued.

"All the time," her friend offered.

I looked over at him wanting desperately to ask if he thought this was his ideal woman: an adult who talks like a elementary student and finds delight in having a rat dance on her head and run around in her long, greasy hair.

"He goes wherever I go. Sometimes, I let him eat off my plate." I threw up a little in my throat.

I knelt down next to the table in hopes of not bringing attention to our interaction. "I appreciate your affection for..."

"Tinker Bell," she offered.

"I was thinking Mickey, but Tinker Bell works," I said. They both chuckled. "I'm sorry, Tinker Bell can't run free in the café."

She was suddenly heartbroken and confused. "Why not?" She said in her whimsical voice.

"Well first of all, we have a company that sets traps for such creatures." She was horrified. "Other customers would not appreciate Tinker Bell's ..." I searched for a word, "specialness. I'm going to have to ask you to put him back in the backpack and not let him out.

"But he can get out by himself, does it all the time," she said.

"Oh, isn't that sweet," I said, still forcing a caring smile. "If that's the case, then I'm going to have to ask you not to bring him in the store."

"What the hell?" the boyfriend responded. "It's her pet."

"I'm sorry," I said, hoping they thought I was speaking to the current situation and not its real intent... that I was sorry they felt a rat was an appropriate pet to bring into a restaurant... or that they thought it was all right to have it crawling around the table. "I don't want to offend you in any way, but I just can't have a rat in my store. I hope you understand."

She gave me the same sweet smile that wrinkled her nose and made her eyes squint. "You can't do that," he started to say. She held out her hand to quiet him.

"It's all right," she softly said. She gently reached up to her shoulder and retrieved Tinker Bell, gave it a gentle kiss on the head and whispered, "Back in your house," and placed him in her back pack.

"Thank you," I offered. She nodded.

I turned to walk back toward the bar and realized that my attempts not to draw attention to the table had failed. Most of those seated in the café were looking in my direction. I continued to force my smile. Renee hadn't moved, and by the time I was standing next to her, Cinderella, her charming prince, and their pet rat were at the door.

"And now, we have a rat lady," I said. Renee just shook her head.

I returned to the back room and was once again sitting at the desk, lost in work, when Jackie returned.

"Are they here yet?" she asked.

I looked at my watch, "Is it 4:00 p.m. already? No, dear, they should be walking in any minute."

A second later the back door flung open and Barry ducked in under the door frame.

"I bet you get tired of that," I said.

"Of what?" he replied.

"Ducking."

"Don't even think about." He turned and looked up at the door, stood straight and walked back out, he barely passed through. Barry turned around and involuntarily ducked back under the door frame. "See, it just happens."

He handed me the FedEx package and returned to the café. I pulled the paper zipper off the back and retrieved the stack of envelopes.

"It's not here," I said. "When did you start?"

"Three weeks ago," Jackie said. "This should be a full check."

I looked through the paychecks again, this time laying each one on the desk after I read the name. When I laid the last one down, I said, "It's not here."

BANG!! I spun around. Jackie had made a fist and hit the center of the refrigerator so violently it made a dent. Barry burst through the back door.

"What the hell was that?" he shouted.

"Nothing," I said, as I kept my eyes on Jackie and shooed him away. "It's OK."

Jackie stood frozen in anger. I don't even think she knew what she had done. The word *psychology* began running though my head. I put both hands on her shoulders and was surprised how solid they were. *She could do some damage*, I thought.

"Jackie, look at me. I'm sorry the check isn't in the pile. It's too late for me to call the office; they are already closed for the weekend. Jackie, look at me." Her eyes shifted. "I can't get you the full amount, but how much do you absolutely need before Tuesday?"

"Why? How are you going to get it if they are closed?" she demanded.

"Just tell me, how much do you need to get you to Tuesday when we can have your check here?" I asked again.

"Three hundred," she said.

"You're sure? Three hundred will cover you?"

"Yes."

"Listen, I'll take care of it. Meet me back here at 4:30 p.m." I squeezed her shoulders before letting them go.

Jackie walked out of the back room in a trance. I grabbed my purse and followed her. Barry was standing just outside the back room door. "Everything all right?" he asked.

"I'm not sure, lot of anger that one... lot of anger."

I got in my car and headed toward the bank. It was a warm, dry fall day, the kind that makes you feel the need to take slow deep breaths. With each breath, the aroma of the fall air and the coffee from my car mingled into the perfect fall potpourri. The sun was shining with no clouds insight. I turned on the radio, Hakuna Matata from The Lion King came on my personalized Disney/Muppet station.

"Call Daniel's cell," I instructed the lady who sits in my dashboard. She respectfully obeyed my commands.

"Hey," he responded.

"Hi!"

"What's up?"

"I have a situation at work, and I'm going to withdraw four hundred dollars."

"Are you OK?"

"They screwed up a paycheck for my new hire, and she is desperate. I'm going to float her money 'till we can have her check here on Tuesday."

"That's a lot to be handing over."

"I think she's good for it. She punched out my refrigerator when her check wasn't with the stack."

"She what?"

"She punched out my fridge, actually dented it."

"Is this the psychology chick?"

"How did you know?"

"You know what they say."

"Yeah, she has issues. Oh, and today, I had a rat in my store."

"In the store?"

"Yep!"

"Didn't know they liked coffee."

I returned in twenty minutes and walked in the back room to find Suzie in her civilian clothes. "So you don't wear coffee clothes all the time?" I said.

"What happened here?" She said pointing to the dented fridge.

"Just a little unresolved anger," I said, as I took the stack of bills and placed them in an envelope.

"Your's?" she asked.

"No," I shook my head and chuckled at the thought.

"Let me guess, Jackie?"

I nodded. With raised eyebrows, Suzie put her finger to her lips, spun around, and beelined toward the door. The back door swung open, and Suzie put her hand over her heart. Jackie entered, and Suzie left with a nod.

I handed Jackie the envelope. "There's four hundred in there. You can pay it back when your check comes," I said.

"Where did this come from?" she asked. "Will you get in trouble?"

"No. And don't worry where it came from. I'll call first thing Monday morning, and we'll get your check fixed."

She opened the envelope and ran her finger across the top of the bills. "Thanks," she said softly.

"My pleasure," I said. "Sorry it even happened in the first place."

"But it's not your fault," she said.

"It may not be, but I offered you the job and promised you would get paid. I have to hold up my end of the bargain."

I watched as Jackie stood motionless, looking down at the money. I wanted to know what was going through her head. The beast who had slugged my defenseless refrigerator had become comatose.

After a long stretch of silence, I said, "Why don't you go pay your bills. There's a little more in there than you said you needed, take yourself out for a burger."

Her expression softened. I sensed that she really wanted to reach out and hug me but didn't know how. I put my arm around her, turned her around, and we walked out of the back room. Entering the café, I stopped and she continued out the door.

"Hey, boss," Barry said as he towered behind me. "She going to be ok?"

"In the short term or long term?" I asked.

"Either," he said.

I looked up at him, way up. "Barry, you never know who's going to enter your world. In this position, you don't know who's going to cross your path, work for you or with you. You have no idea what baggage or experiences they will bring with them. All you can do is be the best you can be and take care of them the best you know how."

He smiled and put his arm around me, "Let me buy you a drink." he said.

"When did we start serving tequila?"

Macchiato
(mah-key-AH-toe)

The macchiato is a cornerstone of Italian coffee culture.

Served in a demitasse cup, this single espresso shot it topped with a small amount of foamed milk. The name macchiato means "marked." So really, you could look at it as a cross between an espresso and a cappuccino.

Since Italians only drink cappuccino in the morning, a macchiato gives the afternoon drinker the option of having a little milk in their espresso.

It's also a good option for those who can't tolerate a strong espresso but find a cappuccino too weak and milky.

16 | Dumpster Diving

Michael, the screenwriter, continued gracing us with his presence. He had become as much a part of the landscape of our store as the leather chair he occupied. He also continued to spend two dollars a day for an endless cup of coffee.

It was midmorning, and I was doing a quick survey of the café when I noticed the leather chair was empty. "Where's the playwright dude?" I asked.

"Michael?" Suzie responded. "He's a scriptwriter, not a playwright--don't know--maybe casting -- can I leave?"

"Why?" I asked.

"Casting! Casting!" she called out cupping her hands around her mouth to send the call out across the café.

"I don't think you fit the part--even if he is writing about us."

"Oh, thanks!" she said looking dramatically dejected.

"She's right here," I heard Renee say as she approached. "Hold on one minute."

"It's for you," she said handing the phone over to me.

"Who is it?" I mouthed. She shrugged her shoulders.

"Thanks," I said rolling my eyes.

"This is Jenn."

"Jenn, this is Michael, the writer guy."

"Hey, Michael, we were just taking about you, your chair is empty."

"I know. I have a favor."

"Sure." My audience leaned in trying to hear the conversation.

"I've misplaced a small notebook. I think it had a black and white cover. There's a scene in there that I've been working on for weeks. They are ready to transcribe it, and I can't find it. Any chance it's there? Oh, please God, let it be there."

"I'm so sorry to hear that, let me look around. I don't recall seeing it but that doesn't mean it's not here. We have a lost and found box...here, give me your number, we'll search and hopefully find it for you."

"Thank you so much. I can't believe I did this. It was perfect, too."

"Don't panic, what's your number?" I jotted down his number and said I'd call him shortly.

"Who was that?" Suzie asked.

"Michael. He's misplaced a notebook and thinks he may have left it here."

"Black and white?" she asked.

"Yes, do we have it?"

"There's been one in the lost and found with a ton of writing in it. No name or number. Been there about a week."

"I cleaned out the lost and found last night. Don't think it's there anymore." Becca said in passing.

"What day is it?" I looked down at my watch hoping it could tell me.

"Tuesday."

"Trash pickup is tomorrow, it could still be out there." I turned toward the back door and motioned to Suzie, "follow me."

"You're going through the trash?" Suzie inquired.

"We are, meaning you and me," pointing at both of us emphasizing my instructions. "We're going through the trash," I clarified.

"Hey, big guy," Suzie yelled out motioning toward Barry. "We're going to need you."

"Good call," I said. "Becca, look through the lost and found and under the counters, let's hope it's here."

Suzie and I walked to the back, scanning the back room as we passed through. "Shit," she said after looking though a stack of files on a shelf over the desk.

"Did you just say a bad word?" I asked.

"Hell, no!" she said.

I scanned the shelves hoping the notebook would reveal itself. "I've done some weird things, but this takes the cake."

"What are we doing?" Barry asked catching up to us.

"We're going to do some garbage diving."

"No way!" he said.

"Way!" Suzie and I said in unison as we nodded our heads.

The dumpster sat just behind our store. Café garbage is beyond dirty. Coffee grounds, unfinished beverages, half-eaten muffins; it's a black, wet mess.

"If the notebook went out last night, let's hope it was in a separate bag. If it's in a bag with coffee grounds, it's probably destroyed."

"What are we looking for?" Barry asked.

"A notebook with a black and white covered," I said.

"It's small, like the ones you get from the dollar store," Suzie said.

"That would make sense, a dollar store notebook for the man who has figured out how to drink great coffee for about the same price," I said.

"That bothers you, doesn't it," Barry said.

"Just a little," I replied.

We began retrieving the clear plastic garbage bags and without opening them, did our best to inspect them. After ten or so bags were piled on the concrete and we could no longer reach the remaining, I looked down at my shoes. "I'll get in," I said.

"In there?" Suzie asked.

"Can you go get the step stool? I'll climb in." I said.

As Suzie retrieved a step stool from the store, Barry and I reinspected the bags we had retrieved. "Think this through," I said. "I'm guessing it would have been the last bag of trash that got thrown on the pile, so it would be the first bag in the dumpster. It's down there. I'm sure it is."

I climbed up the step stool, pulled my legs over the edge of the dumpster, and sat on the ledge. "Gardyloo," I shouted as I dropped myself down.

"What's that?"

"It's what the peasants used to say to warn people below as they threw slop out the windows, "Gardyloo!"

My feet landed on the uneven surface, and the bags squished. I pulled several bags up and began stacking them in the corner of the dumpster. "You guys all right out there?" Renee called from the back door.

"Jenn's doing her Christmas shopping," Suzie yelled back.

"I got it!" I shouted grabbing a bag that looked as if it only contained paper. "Here, open it." I tossed it out of the dumpster. My accomplices tore it open. "Please let it be in there."

As they sorted through the papers, I stepped on another bag and crunched. "Well, that's broken," I said as if it mattered. I reached down and picked up the bag.

"We're not finding it," Suzie said.

I tore open the crunched bag and began scanning its contents. At the very bottom was a thick stack of papers covered in coffee grounds. I turned the bag upside down to avoid sticking my hand in the grime. As I did, I saw the black and white diagonal-striped notebook. "I think I've found it."

I pulled the notebook out and handed it to Barry, who was hanging as far over the edge of the dumpster as he could. "It's dirty," I said.

Barry grabbed it and began hitting it against the dumpster in an attempt to remove the coffee. He began thumbing through it. "This looks like it, there's a lot of writing in here. I can see why he was panicked."

"Suzie, go call him and tell him we have it. Apologize for its condition. And don't tell him how we found it."

"Why not?"

"When he's rich and famous, we'll tell him the story. It will mean more then," I said.

Suzie took the notebook and headed inside.

"And after you call him, don't keep the number. No matter how many times you say it, he isn't your type."

Without turning around, Suzie gave me the finger and entered the store.

"How are you going to get out of there, boss?" Barry asked.

"Good question," I said. "Didn't think this all the way through, did I?"

"Here, try and find some even ground to put the step-stool on," he said offering me the stool.

"But how will we get it out?" I asked.

"Good thinking."

I walked over to the mound of discarded bags and began to climb up. They gave me enough support to get close enough to the top to pull myself up to the ledge. Barry offered his hand and I finished the descent.

We tossed the examined bags back into the dumpster and returned to the back room.

"I think I need a shower," I said. "That was disgusting."

"Why don't you go home boss," Barry said. "Take a stink day."

"A stink day! That's awesome," I said as I fast forwarded the day ahead. "Think you can handle it?"

"Sure. Piece of cake," he said.

"I think I will." I washed my hands and grabbed my bag. "I'll go out the back, I don't want to walk through the café looking like Pig Pen from Charlie Brown. Can you lock the door behind me?"

"No problem."

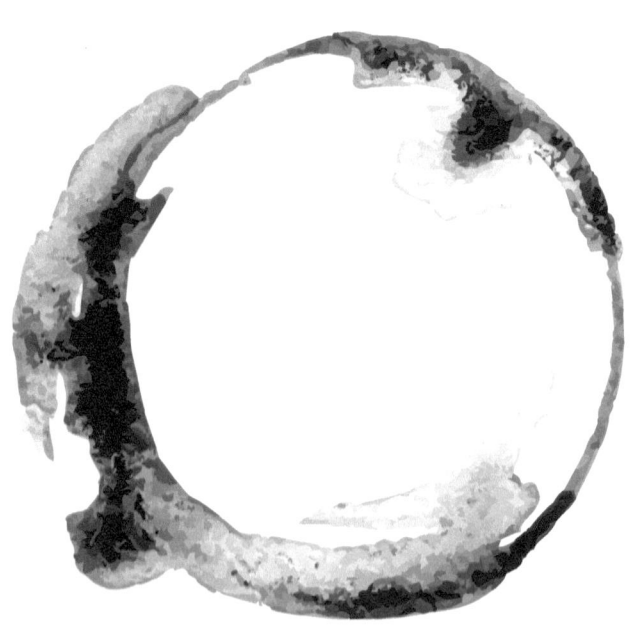

From Green to Yum!

All coffee begins as a green bean.

At 200 - 250 degrees f. it begins to turn yellow.

At 250 - 300 degrees f. it becomes light brown.

Between 395 - 405 degrees f. the first pop is heard. This means the moisture is being removed and the bean is expanding.

City Roast, the lightest roast, is achieved at 425 - 435 degrees f.

Full City Roast is achieved at 450 degrees f. and the beginning of the second pop is heard.

Espresso Roast is achieved at 455 - 465 degrees f.

French Roast is achieved at 470 - 490 degrees f.

Spanish Roast is achieved at 520 - 530 degrees f.

Next phase - flames!

17 | Café Life
Back Room Interactions

"They're swamped out there!" Gregg announced as he entered the back room.

I jumped to my feet, grabbed my apron, "nice to see you," I said, as I passed him and bolted through the door expecting to find a mob of people surrounding the bar. Instead, I was greeted with the normal afternoon line.

"They're fine," I said turning back.

"I know, just wanted your desk," he said taking my seat and emptying his briefcase.

"Someday you may be important enough to have a desk of your own," I said.

"Perhaps," he said. "How are things?"

"You tell me."

He picked up a stack of reports and began scanning through them. "Yep, things look all right."

"Someday, I hope to hear the word "good" rather than all right, but for today, I'll take that as a compliment."

Gregg pulled out his laptop, a stack of file folders, and his phone. "Hey, do you recognize this guy?" He began scrolling through the photos on the phone.

"Those your kids?" I asked as he scrolled through family photos.

"Yeah."

"Wow, they're cute," I said. "Are they your stepkids?"

"Bitch!" he said without looking up. "Here he is." He stopped on an image of a man sitting at a high top table in one of our stores. "Do you recognize him?"

"Yeah, from here, right?" I took the phone to observe closer. "He's in here midmorning."

"Alone?"

"Not usually... a blond, I think."

"Her?" He scrolled to the next picture.

"No, don't recognize her. Why? Who is she?"

"What about her?" He handed me back the phone while pointing to a woman in the next image.

"No, don't think so. Wow, she has really big hair! There could be things living in there." I drew the phone closer and then handed it back to Gregg. "Are you going to expand on this interesting conversation about nothing?"

"From what I can gather, this guy visits three stores and has a different woman with him in each."

"No way... secretaries?"

"Or...."

"Wait, let me see him again," I grabbed the phone back and held it closer, scrolling back through the pictures. "I don't know, he doesn't look like...oh, maybe... it's them, they kinda do."

"Assistants?" Gregg asked with a smirk.

"Ahh, I don't know. That's a job I'll never have, an assistant. I never want a job with the word ass in it... can't be good."

"You'll never be an assistant... or an ASSISTANT?"

"Neither! Unless I can use the back room. I hear it's all the rage. Heard from your buddy Kenneth lately?"

"Not since the day I fired his sorry ass."

"Did you enjoy that one?"

"Just a little."

I returned to the phone photo. "You said three stores? All in one day?"

"I'm not sure, it's not like I'm following him."

"What, no PI Gregg? Why not? What else do you have to do?"

He began to respond but was interrupted by Suzie's theatrical entrance. Her hands were outstretched in front of her and she began singing, "I have everything that I need...right in front of me...." She finished and bowed as if she was on stage. Although we offered no applause, I was sure she heard it in her head.

"Hey, do you recognize him?" I handed Suzie the phone.

"What, no applause?" She took the phone and held it close to her face. "The hazelnut latte, extra hot? And she gets... skinny, sugar free vanilla with extra whip cream."

I looked at Gregg, "there's your answer. That's why I keep her around. She knows every customer and sings Muppet songs." I sensed Suzie's eagerness to hear the rest of the story by the snapping of her fingers.

"Gregg says he visits three stores regularly and meets a different woman at each."

"All in the same day?"

"That's yet to be determined." I retrieved the phone from her hand. "Whatcha need?" I asked.

"More Devil's Candy..."

"Devil's Candy? What the hell is that?" Gregg asked. I burst out laughing from his expression. He had become a little trigger happy since the Kenneth ordeal.

"Not to worry. It's just Chocolate Covered Espresso Beans," I explained.

"It's my *sale of the day*," Suzie said. Gregg looked at me for further clarification.

"She picks one item every day and sees how many she can sell," I said.

"We're out of them out there, any more back here?"

"On the last shelf on the right," I said pointing in the direction.

"Kari bought a bag," she said walking to the back corner.

"Kari?" Giving her my...*please tell me what she drinks so I know who we are talking about...* tone.

"You know, the ex-large latte with an extra shot of coffee."

"Shot of coffee?" Gregg asked, giving us his...*what the hell is that?...* look again.

"She thinks an extra shot of espresso would be too much, so she gets a shot of coffee in it. Whatever, we just give them what they ask for," Suzie said, waving her hands in the air.

"And she bought a bag of beans?" he asked.

"Magical beans," Suzie clarified with a twinkle in her eye.

"Did you warn her?" I asked.

"I did," she said, as she filled her arms with a pile of small cellophane bags tied with pretty gold ribbons.

"Look, we make them look so innocent. So pretty. Pretty little chocolates..."

"The first one is always free," Suzie said as she exited.

"So, what are we going to do about the man with too many coffee buddies?" I asked.

"Nothing," Gregg said. "Just think it's interesting."

"Hey, Jenn," Renee said as she pushed the door open. "The rat lady is back! Oh, Hi Gregg. When did you get here?"

"Been here since you opened," he said. "The rat lady?"

"Oh, that's nice," she said.

"She's back," I said failing miserably to keep my cool. "Where is she?" I said taking a step toward the door.

Renee reached out and grabbed my arm, "She's not here, just wanted to see your reaction."

"Thanks," I said and took a deep breath to shake off the rage that had already begun to well up.

"Everyone's been signed off on their coffee knowledge. Now what do you want to do?" She paused for a moment. "Except you!" She said addressing Gregg. "I came in at eight and you weren't here."

"Coffee knowledge? Rat lady?" Gregg asked. "Now, what are you all doing?"

"Go ahead, tell him. It's your baby," I instructed.

"About both?" Renee asked. I nodded.

"We've spent the last eight weeks expanding our coffee knowledge, from origins to flavor profiles to degrees of roasting. Jenn wanted everyone to be tested, and I just finished the last one," Renee said.

"Nice," he said, nodding his head in rare approval.

"Let me think about it, but for sure we need to make it part of every shift so everyone feels like an expert." I hit Gregg on the shoulder. "Describe Sumatra," I said.

He hesitated for a moment until he realized I was serious-- "an Indonesian coffee, full bodied and earthy with a hint of chocolate."

"I'm impressed," Renee said. She looked at me, "Describe Mocha-Java."

"The first known blended coffee. Both African coffees from the ports of Mocha and Java, full bodied, earthy with hints of raisin, cinnamon and tobacco, containing no mocha," I said shaking my finger.

"Now, the rat lady?" he asked.

"I'll tell you about her later, when Jenn's not around. Hey, why is the 'ex-large hazelnut latte, extra hot' guy on your phone?" Renee asked looking at Gregg's phone now lying on the desk.

"You better erase those," I said.

"So why is he...?" she asked again.

"It appears our ex-large, extra hot latte has a string of women he meets at our stores. Gregg was just asking if he comes here as well."

"And you took a picture of him? That's creepy," she said.

Gregg picked up the phone and deleted each picture. "Feel better?" he asked.

"Not really," she said. "Still kinda creepy."

The door flew open hard enough to slam against the back wall with a thud. "You better get something to eat!" Suzie said to the person on the phone. "No, you can't die." She looked up at me, "She can't die, can she?"

I shook my head, "Who?"

"No, you can't die, that's only dogs. Just stop and get some food. Oh, and drink a lot of water. We don't call them the Devil's Candy for nothing. See you tomorrow. Good idea, you better dry out a day. Drive safe."

"Is it any wonder I can't get anything done back here," I said. "Who was that?"

"Kari."

"The Devil's Candy chick from this morning?" I asked.

"They're doing construction on Hwy. 1, and she's been sitting for about an hour...said she opened the bag and couldn't stop eating them...she has quite the buzz."

"She ate the whole bag in one sitting?"

"Almost."

"That would be quite the buzz," Renee said. "We should sample those out one day. You know the first one is always free."

"As much as I'm enjoying our conversations, I have to be on the bar in an hour and I still have things to do." I looked at Suzie, "You ready?"

"If I have to," she said.

"Ready for what?" Gregg asked.

"To learn the bar," I said without thinking.

"Wait, learn the bar?"

The cat was out of the bag. I began backpeddling as quickly as I could, but I knew this wasn't going to go over well. "Did I say that? No, she just needs to be certified on a few drinks. Nothing you need to worry about, I got this covered." I hoped that he would drop it. Suzie had been with us for far too long not to be working the bar. It was a minor detail that I felt didn't need to be revealed. "Did you know we had a rat in here?--changing the subject.

"Did you call someone?" he asked.

"No," Renee said. "She just asked it to leave."

"And did it?" he asked.

"Yes," I said nodding my head…"was very accommodating. I really have some things I need to get done." I reached across the desk and gathered the papers that I had been working on before Gregg's entrance. "I'll go find a table out in the café. Do you need me for anything?" I asked Gregg.

"You asked the rat to leave?" he asked.

"Yes, I did and yes, it left," I said with no explanation. "Now, do you need me for anything?"

No," he replied.

"Good," I said collecting the last file folder.

"I'll join you," Gregg said collecting his laptop.

"You couldn't have just done that in the first place?" I asked.

I turned toward the door the same moment Barry came flying through it. "We have to either get rid of him or get rid of this song," he said more flustered than I had ever seen him.

"Get rid of who?" I asked.

"Jess. Two days ago when this song came on he asked if he could have a moment. I said sure, then he stood in the middle of the bakery with his eyes closed until the song was over."

"What song is playing?" I asked.

"American Pie," Barry replied.

"You mean the *bye, bye Miss American pie, drove the Chevy to the levy and the levy was dry*…American Pie?" Renee asked.

"The very one," Barry said.

"That's a 15 minute song!" Gregg interrupted. "That's an entire break."

"I know," Barry said rolling his eyes. "Guess who just stood in the middle of the café, eyes closed and swaying to the music for the last 15 minutes?" Barry asked while giving us his best imitation of Jess.

"Did you ask him why he likes that song so much? Seems weird. He's too young to have that kind of attachment," I added.

"No, I didn't ask," Barry said with a smirk. "I'm assuming that would be another 15-minute explanation. It's like when people ask if I've seen a movie and I just say 'yes' so I don't have to listen to them tell me about it."

"What!" Renee said putting her hands on her hips. "Do you do that when I ask you about movies?"

Barry's smirk turned to a sheepish smile. "Sometimes," he said.

Renee sighed, "I thought you and I liked the same kind of movies." Barry's smile turned into a frown and he hung his head sadly.

"Well, I don't think we can get one song out of our music rotation, but we can get our employee to understand, that he can't stop every time it comes on?" Gregg was looking directly at me.

"Yes, I believe we can do that," I assured him.

I walked out of the back room and into the café just as six older women with big floppy sun hats walked through on their way to the patio, canvases under one arm and large supply satchels under the other. The music track had stopped and a guitar player was playing his rendition of "Moon River" from the back corner, the barista was calling out a drink order, Jess was back behind the bakery counter filling a cookie jar and our man with too many coffee buddies was at the counter ordering "an ex-large hazelnut latte extra-hot and anything that the lady would like."

Limited Time Offer

Sulawesi
$16.95 pound

A bold-bodied coffee from Indonesia. Spicy yet smooth, balanced with bright citrus flavors.

A complex cup.

18 | Bar Fear

The espresso machine can be quite intimidating; Suzie was scared to death of it. She knew all the drink recipes and quality standards. She was an expert--except for the fact that she never made them. If Suzie ever found herself alone, she could make her own drink, but her preference was to be served. This didn't surprise me since during our first conversation she admitted that she was a "sit on the deck and drink margaritas" gal, not a "get down below and scrape barnacles" kind of gal.

Suzie had all the baristas convinced that she was responsible for "on the spot drink quality testing," which meant needing to time them making *her* drink. Suzie was worth her weight in gold when she was on the register, by far the best salesperson ever! But she had been at the Inkwell for more than five months, and she had to conquer this fear. At the very least, to be able to cover the bar during slow times.

Suzie leaned up against the divider that separated the bar from the registers. "All right, show me how it's done," she said.

"Good try," I said. "Get over here and learn this." She held onto the divider as if being sucked into it, forcing herself to let go, and two steps later, she was standing next to me. "You're going to start off by frothing the milk. I'll prep the cups, add the shots, you'll finish them off. I'm going to tell you everything you need to do. Ready? What am I saying? Let's go!"

She nodded. It was rare to see her so focused; there were no theatrics, no song and dance, not even a joke. "Get the practice milk pitcher, the one with the black lines drawn on it; you know, the one you made for everyone else to use." She looked through the assortment of pitchers and retrieved the marked one. "That's the line you fill to," I said pointing to the mark. "That's enough milk for two lattes." Suzie filled the pitcher.

"Put it under the wand and turn on the steam." She did as directed, staring down into the pitcher. "You'll need the thermometer." She let go of the pitcher with one hand, reached into the water well retrieving one of eight thermometoers that lived there, and clipped it to the side. "What temp are you taking it to?" I asked.

"Between 180 and 190," she said.

"What happens at 200?" I asked.

"It's burnt."

"Good! See, you know this," I ensured.

As she continued watching the milk being swirled around the pitchers, I prepped the cups for the next orders and began pulling espresso shots. "What's your temp?" I asked.

"140."

"Bring the pitcher down, let the wand stay right at the top and start frothing."

Suzie pulled the pitcher too far down, and the wand head became exposed resulting in warm milk spitting out of the pitcher and all over her. "You'll only do that once," I said. My sidekick was stone-faced, concentrating on the milk. *Hope she doesn't have a stroke over this*, I thought.

"Can you hear that?" I asked. "That's the frothing sound. Put the wand further in and listen." She did so and the sound softened. "Bring it back to the top," Suzie pulled the pitcher down until the wand was once again resting just below the surface. "Hear the difference?" She nodded. "Froth away 'till you reach your temp."

"When the thermometer reaches 183," I said, "turn the wand off. Don't pull it out before you turn it off or we'll have another milk shower." Again, Suzie did as instructed and set the pitcher on the counter accompanied with a loud sigh as she wiped her brow. "That's perfect," I said. "Look at all that frothy perfection!"

She wiped her hands on her apron and patted her forehead with the sleeve of her shirt. I had only seen her this nervous on her first day at the register, when she began to sweat and shake as I walked her through ringing up a customer.

"Grab a spoon. When you are pouring, you want to hold back the froth to make sure you are getting enough milk in the cup. Once you've added the correct amount of milk, you can free the froth." I watched as she ever so carefully poured the milk into the cup. "OK, open it up." Suzie removed the spoon, which was damming the froth, and it rolled out onto the top of the beverage. "Perfect. Taste it, lid it, and call it out."

"Taste it?" Suzie shouted out.

"Shhhh," I put my finger up to my lips. "I'm kidding--lid it and call it."

"What am I calling?" she asked. She was so focused that the joke never sank in.

"This is a perfect latte, the next has vanilla."

We did this for the next forty-five minutes--each time Suzie became more and more confident. By the end of the forty-five minutes, she was relaxed and back to her normal self, that is, until I said, "It's time to switch." I got a look of disdain. "Don't worry, you can do this."

We swapped positions. "Look at the next order on the screen, pull your cup, add the extras. Now, pull the shot." Suzie took the port-a-filter from the machine and placed it under the espresso grinder. She pulled the lever on the side and a small dose of ground espresso dropped down. She pulled it again and then put the small metal basket, filled with espresso, under the tamping arm and pressed the grounds down-- finally, replacing it back into the machine. "Let's time this one to see if we're calibrated." As she hit the express button, she pressed the red button on a small timer that permanently sat on top of the espresso machine. "How many seconds should it be?" I asked.

"40," she said.

"I don't know why this intimidates you so much, you know all the answers," I said. "If it's over 40 seconds, what does it mean?"

"That the espresso is ground too fine."

"Yep. And if it's 30?" I asked.

"Too coarse," Suzie said.

"Exactly. Think of sand and rocks..."

"Water runs through rocks--or coarse ground--quickly but takes longer to move through sand-- fine ground," Suzie said, finishing my instructions.

"What else prevents it from brewing properly?" I asked.

"Grounds could be packed up in the machine."

"And then what do we do?"

"Back flush to get them cleaned out." She responded with confidence.

"Perfect." I filled the cup with the desired amount of milk and called the order. "Oh crap, I forgot to get those numbers, take over, I'll be right out."

Suzie nodded and I stepped away from the bar, "You're going to be fine," I said... "One drink at a time."

I walked into the back room and turned to watch through the window. Suzie completed the next five drinks perfectly as I watched from a distance.

"OK, I'm back. What can I help you with?" I asked.

"Nothing, I've got this," she said, focused on a pitcher of milk.

"You sure?"

"Yes."

"I'll stay right here, let me know if you need anything." I hung back and began the prep work for the evening shift. Suzie worked for another hour and a half by herself on the bar. It was a huge accomplishment for her. As her shift came to the end, I stepped next to her as she completed the next order.

"You're done!" I said. "You did it."

She looked over at me; I wasn't sure what was coming. "I never want to do that again," she announced.

"But you could if you had to," I said.

"Only if the last living barista on the planet was dead."

"OK, then. Keep that option open. Good job. You can hang out at the register from now on."

"Good," she said, expressionless and visibly exhausted.

As Suzie walked away from the bar, I put my hands on either side of the espresso machine. "Don't listen to her," I said patting the sides. "She can be a bitch sometimes. I love you. I'll always choose you over the registers."

"I heard that..." Suzie said as she walked into the back room.

"I thought you would..."

Order Now!

Order your bakery for
Thanksgiving!

Order forms and more information
at the bakery counter.

Orders must be placed by
November 24th.

Inkwell Cafe

19 | Turkey & Coffee

"I call this meeting to order!" Barry said, as he plopped a platter of fresh pastries and breads in the center of our corner table on the patio.

"Yum, what's all this?" Stephanie asked.

"Samples for Thanksgiving."

"What's that one?" Renee pointed to what I assumed was a pumpkin muffin.

"Pumpkin, cream cheese," Barry replied.

"Where's the cream cheese?" I asked.

"Inside," he said sticking his finger into the middle of one.

"NO!"

"YES!" he said. I grabbed a knife and cut it open. A glob of warm cream cheese oozed out of the center.

"OMG, that looks amazing!" I said.

"Wait 'till you taste it," he said.

"Who cares how it tastes, the presentation is enough to cover any sin."

"You can't start without me," Suzie said setting her normal tray of tasting cups and French presses on the table.

"Coffee and fresh muffins," I said. "This is the best job in the world."

"What are we tasting today Roast Master?"

"Three very similar yet distinct profiles: Guatemala, Sulawesi, and Papua New Guinea."

"Those are my three favorites!" I said.

"Are they really?"

"Yes. You didn't know that?" Renee shook her head. "It's like a Thanksgiving miracle!" I exclaimed.

"Suzie, if you please, pour us some Guatemala. Barry, got any blueberry muffins today?"

"There's a few left," Barry said.

"Mind grabbing one and sampling it out?"

"Not at all," he said getting up. Barry returned with a blueberry muffin cut into six pieces.

"Although Guatemala is a South American coffee, it is considered to be full-bodied, with deep berry notes and a peppery finish, a very complex cup. Let's start with aroma," Renee instructed. We all inhaled. "Now taste."

"I always feel like I'm in church taking communion when we get to this part."

"This would be awesome communion! We should suggest it to Father Mark next time he's in."

"All right, let us drink together," Renee said waving her hand over the table as if she was blessing us.

"Mmmm, so good!" I said from my coffee happy place.

"Let's pair this up with the blueberry muffin. Take a bite of muffin and then a sip of the Guatemala." Renee suggested. We did as instructed.

"Holy Shit!" Barry said.

"And that is why this isn't a good idea for communion," I said.

"That is amazing!"

"Isn't it crazy how all the flavors seem to jump out of the coffee?"

"We need to do more of this with our customers," I said. "We need to get in the habit of having sample cups and paired bakery at the counter. Can you two work on that?" Barry and Renee nodded.

"Ready for the next?" Suzie poured the Sulawesi; a cousin to Sumatra but a bit less in body, with a peppery aroma yet a sweet, bright, citrus flavor. "I'm thinking it may go well with the pumpkin muffin."

We paired the two together and as always, Renee was right. The spiciness of the Sulawesi exploded in our mouths.

"Finally, let's go for the Papua New Guinea. This has a smooth vanilla aroma, soft body with hints of dried cherry and apricot, with a peppery finish.

"Pay close attention, we only have this for a short time. We want to push it for the special coffee at Thanksgiving. It's a great gift as well as a great offering for the meal," Suzie instructed.

"November is a huge month for us," I began. "Barry has made pre-order forms to hand out so customers can place orders for Thanksgiving; pastries for breakfast, breads for dinner, and he's even doing full size pies for desserts." Barry passed a sample of the order form around the table.

"We've got to be on top of this," he said. "I can handle the production, but we need to make sure every order gets to me. Last thing we want is to have someone show up for their Thanksgiving Day order and there not be one."

"Take us through the process, please," I said. "Suzie, you're an important player. If those at the register aren't sure how this works, it's going to fail."

Barry proceeded to walk us through the process covering every detail.

"Let me say in advance, thanks for giving up your holiday. Thanksgiving week is going to be crazy. Barry plans to be here at 4:00 a.m. Wednesday morning to bake off what is being picked up on that day, and at 5:00 a.m. on Thanksgiving to bake off that day's orders as well as what we'll need for our regular day. The schedule is written; we begin 5:00 a.m. Thanksgiving, and we don't close until midnight on Friday." "How many hours is that?" Barry asked and we all began counting on our fingers.

"I get forty-two," Suzie said with raised brow.

"Sounds about right," added Renee.

I let out a sign. It sounded like an enourmous amount of time to me. "I'm not expecting us to be too busy during the night, but we should have a steady flow of those shopping all night. Stephanie is canvassing the mall with pre-order forms for any store who wants us to deliver coffee and bakery on black Friday."

"Do we have enough staff for this?" Suzie asked.

"I hope so," I said. "I'll get everyone's confirmation on the schedule by the end of the week--after that, no changes...and no one gets sick! If you're puking, we'll keep you in the back room close to a bucket, but we'll find something for you to do. Everyone has to stay healthy," I insisted pounding my fist on the table. "We can all die on Saturday, wait, I take that back. ... on Monday, not before."

"Are the other stores doing all of this?" Renee asked.

"Not all of them," I said.

"Are we telling them what we're doing?" added Barry.

"Not all. We'll wait 'till it's successful, then we'll tell them."

"And if it's not?" Renee asked.

"They will never know."

"That's how we roll here at the Inkwell," Suzie said.

"Excuse me," a deep voice interrupted. I turned. "This is for you, all of you." It was Michael, the screenwriter. He had the largest gift basket I had ever seen in his hands. We cleared a corner and he set it down.

"This is beautiful!" Barry said.

"It's done," Michael announced.

"The screenplay?" I asked. He nodded. We all stood and applauded, and Michael took a bow.

"Congratulations!" I said.

"Couldn't have done it without you guys. Thanks for everything, for my leather chair and bottomless coffee, and especially for finding the lost notebook. It was a godawful mess, but at least it was, and I am ever so grateful."

"We'll tell you the real story sometime," Suzie said.

"What?" His tone and expression instantly changing.

"Nevermind. When it's a box office hit, we'll fill you in," I said.

"Speaking of, I was in Hollywood last week, they are going ahead with casting, and shooting begins next summer. I think we can have a screening downtown in the little theater when production is done."

"That would be awesome!" Barry said.

"Can you tell us what it's about?" I asked.

"No, I will tell you it takes place in an insane asylum--I got a lot of insight watching your customers."

We burst into laughter. "So it is about us!" Suzie laughed.

Michael made his way around the table, shaking hands and sharing hugs. When he finished saying goodbye to the last of us, he once again took a bow, and we applauded and then he left. We applauded him all the way out the door. It was as if we were sending our child out into the big world. We all felt sad and a little bit lonely when he left. The leather chair that had been his home since we opened was now available for a new vision, a new project, a new courageous soul with a dream.

I ordered a small brass plaque the next day to be placed on the back of the chair; it simply read "Michael's Chair." After all this time, that is all we knew about him, that his name was Michael, he wrote a screenplay, and he sat in our chair.

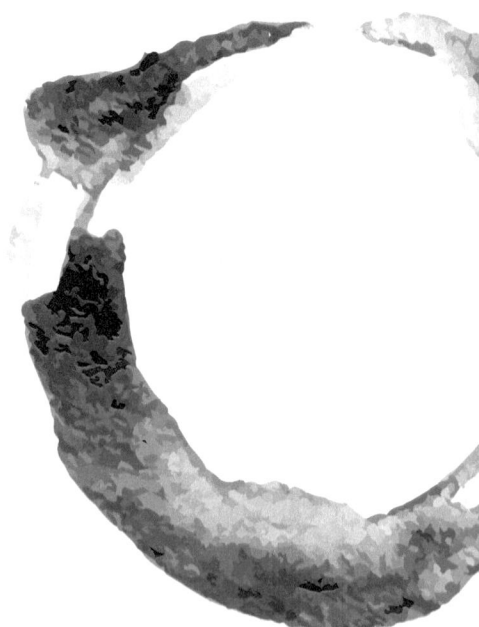

HOW MUCH COFFEE?

A coffee tree produces an average of one and a half to two pounds of coffee per year. That represents from 3 to 4 thousand hand picked coffee cherries and 6 to 8 thousand coffee beans.

That's 1.5 pounds yield per tree, per year. 2.4 billion pounds of coffee are sold annually in the U.S. alone. That means that approximately 1.6 billion trees are required annually just to supply the U.S.

When people say it's a small world, well it just makes you wonder.

One shot of espresso uses approximately 45 coffee beans.

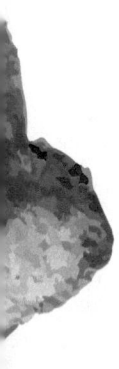

20 | Turkey Day

Thanksgiving came quickly; we were as prepared as we knew how to be. Barry had an overwhelming response to the pre-ordering bakery idea, forcing us to rethink how we could get it all done; 3:00 a.m. Thanksgiving morning was the scheduled time. Holidays in a café are different from most retailers--no one rushing in for big screen televisions, no hot deals. Most customers make their appearance after they've filled their cars with all their purchases and need a place to sit and unwind. It's when our customers are on their best behavior and are extremely thankful that we are there.

I worked a split shift this Thanksgiving. I greeted our morning customers, then headed home for an afternoon scaled down turkey dinner, only to return that evening. Uncertain how busy we would be through the night, I had made a list of tasks to be done in order to prep for the next day. The slower than expected stream of customers allowed us to get through the list quickly.

Toward the bottom of the list read Make mocha. Our mocha was shipped to us in twenty-five pound boxes. Inside was a double thick plastic bag filled with twenty-five pounds of cocoa powder. Making mocha is a dirty job. It's hard not to spill some of the powder and impossible not to let the powder escape into the air.

Becca was running though the list getting the prep done when she came to the Make Mocha line.

"How much are we making?" she asked.

"Let's do the whole box," I said.

"How many batches is that?" she asked.

"I think six, but don't do it in individual batches. Get a plastic tub and let's mix it all at once."

"Are you sure that works?"

"No, but it should...a lot easier than mixing six batches."

"Ok," she said with great hesitation as she entered the back room.

Her response made me rethink the instructions. I stayed out front thinking through the process. "It should work. If she opens the box and pours the powder into the tub, then add...." I spun around and shoved open the back door, "Don't dump it in all at..." is what I got out just in time to watch her pick up the plastic bag and begin dumping it into the bucket.

A billow of mocha powder erupted out of the tub and filled the back room. We both began coughing and fanning our noses searching for clean air. Renee walked up behind me, all she saw were two figures being consumed by a dark cloud of mocha. "This isn't good," she said calmly.

It took some time for the powder to settle and when it did, it was everywhere. A thin layer of cocoa powder not only covered the back room, it covered us. Our arms were brown, our faces were covered and so were our clothes. "Well, we won't do that again," I said.

We laughed and began cleaning up. We wiped off everything with mocha on it, but I knew more was hiding in every crack and crevasse in the back room. Once we had most of it cleaned up, Becca added the warm water to the bucket of powder and we watched it slowly turn into thick, dark mocha syrup.

As midnight approached, I began gathering my things to leave. I watched the clock tick by, waiting for Barry to arrive to cover the night shift. "You smell all chocolaty," he said as he walked into the back room.

"It's Charlie's Chocolate Factory back here," I said. "We're going to smell chocolate for a long time."

"Good to know," he said. "Any last instructions?"

"No, you should have time to get a lot done tonight, been a steady stream of customers, but nothing overwhelming-- should be a good night."

"Be careful going home, fog's coming in," he said.

"Thanks. Hope it's not foggy tomorrow."

I collected my bag, said goodbye to the team and stepped outside. Barry was right, the fog was rolling in off the ocean. By the time I got to the car, the smell of mocha grew stronger. I looked down at my arm, the moisture in the air was mixing with the powder on my skin and little brown rivers began flowing toward my hands.

"The fog," I said. "I'm turning into mocha."

I got in the car and looked in the mirror. My face seemed to be a few shades darker. I looked quite scary in the shadows of the parking lot lights. I started the car and pulled out of the lot. The quickest and most direct route home includes five miles on a two-lane road that runs along the nature preserve. Trees line the road, and shrubs stretch out to the edge of the pavement.

My mind likes to hang onto scary events. Unfortunately, it rarely differentiates between real and fictional events. When I was a kid, I watched an episode of Hawaii Five-O where the killer hid in the bushes whispering, "pretty girl, pretty girl," just before he killed them. I heard that voice for the next ten years behind bushes, in closets, under beds, basically anywhere it was dark. More recently, I walked into the living room one night where Daniel was watching a particularly frightening episode of the X-files. I have no idea what the story was, only that there was a scary-looking creature peering into the review mirror from the back seat of Scully's car. "Oh God," I recall saying, "Now that's going to stay in my head."

When I turned onto the nature preserve road, I made the mistake of glancing in the mirror and saw a dark, now streaking face, looking back at me. I was almost unrecognizable with mocha running down my face from my forehead. The darkness of the night and the eerie glow from the lights of the dashboard turned my reflection into a creepy mocha creature. The X-files theme began to play in my head with full orchestration and sound effects. As I turned the corner, something in the back seat shifted.

"Shit! There's someone in the back seat! BUT don't look in the mirror!" The night seemed darker than usual and the trees were swallowing the road. The fog added a layer of mystery, and all I could smell was mocha. "Don't look in the mirror! Roll down the windows!" I did. The more the wind blew into the car, the more the fog saturated my clothing and the wetter and more chocolaty I became.

"Sing!" I instructed myself, so I did. "The wheels on the bus go round and round, round and round, round and round... Is this road ever going to end? Don't look in the mirror, you're too scary! ...all over town. The wipers on the bus go swish, swish, swish, swish, swish, swish, swish swish ... If there's someone in the back seat feel free to join in ... the wheels on the bus go round and round... and if you're here to kidnap me, I promise I really am this crazy, ...all over town...Don't be fooled by the smell, I'm not nice... swish, swish, swish..."

It was the longest five miles I had ever driven. When I finally reached the end and turned under a street light, I caught a glimpse of myself in the mirror. I had streaks of chocolate running the full length of my face. I could have won an Academy Award for best make-up in the horror category. By now my clothes had become liquid chocolate, and I felt it running down my legs. When we lived in the south, we had heard of snakes slithering into empty cars and curling up under the seat. I was sure one had done just that and was now licking the mocha from my leg.

"Daniel!" I shouted, "Why have you made me move all over tarnation?" I began pounding my foot on the floor in hopes of keeping the snakes at bay. Something else shifted in the back seat. "Maybe the snake will eat the stranger crouched back there."

"I just want to get home!" I yelled at the top of my lungs. I didn't care who heard me. If I was lucky enough for it to be a cop, he could follow me home, or at least kill the snake that I felt licking the chocolate off my legs, while he arrested the stranger lurking in the back seat.

The street lights were getting closer together and although the roadway seemed brighter, the lighting created more shadows and movement within the car. As I made the last turn before my driveway, the unknown stranger in the backseat once again shifted.

"No one will ever believe me," I said as I pulled into the driveway, opening my door before coming to a complete stop and feeling somehow less trapped. I leaped out of the car as soon as I turned off the ignition. I forced myself to look in the back windows searching for the stranger I was sure was crouched down behind me; there was no one. As I turned around, my eyes caught a glimpse of the front seat, where I saw a brown outline of myself on the driver's seat. It was the mocha version of chalk marks that outline dead bodies.

"It already smells like coffee, now it's going to smell like mocha. We're going to be smelling mocha for a long time." I ran into the house before the family of raccoons, that I was sure were looking down at me from the magnolia tree, decided to pin me to the ground and lick off all the chocolate.

Story Reading

& hot cocoa by the

fireplace

Every weekday at
11:00 a.m.
Now through Dec. 21st.

Inkwell Cafe

21 | A Gray and Red Christmas

The team at the café somehow survived Thanksgiving weekend, no one got sick, no one missed a beat. There was hardly time to take a breath as December rolled in. We had recently been put on high alert. The CEO of the company was touring the West Coast and would be visiting stores. He didn't make known his schedule, he preferred unannounced visits.

It was a regular Tuesday morning, the rush was over, and we were recovering from a busy morning. Stephanie had arranged for a group of children to visit the store, make hot chocolate, and listen to stories while drinking hot chocolate around the fireplace. Twenty small paper cups lined the back counter along with a tray of tiny cookies.

Stephanie and Becca had developed a great working relationship. They were opposites in every aspect of their real life, but somehow were great buddies at work. Stephanie was tall, slim, blond hair, blue eyes, with a strong German accent, married to a soon-to-be-doctor. Becca was just shy of five feet, was almost as wide as she was tall, especially around the hips. She had black hair, wore black framed glasses, and her husband was hoping for a promotion to assistant manager at Jiffy Lube. Two opposite worlds coming together at the Inkwell, and you would have thought they had known each other all their lives.

Becca was getting ready to fill several canisters of whipped cream before the children arrived. Whipped cream canisters are made of almost indestructible steel. They are thin cylinders that stand about a foot high. When filled with cold whipped cream, they become a torpedo that could take out any uninvited guest. I have walked through many empty back rooms holding tightly to its handle ready to swing at any intruder's head.

Stephanie was behind the counter finishing the drink preparation when a thin man wearing a grey sweatshirt and pants walked in. He stopped as he entered and then shuffled over toward the bar.

"Hello," I said. "Can I help you?"

"Jenn," he said holding out his hand.

"Yes," I reached out and shook his hand. Images in my head flew past as I tried to remember how he knew me.

"It's John, John Banner."

John Banner, the CEO of our company, John Banner? The big boss, the one who started this place? "John," I said reaching out my hand, "I didn't recognize you. Everything all right?"

"I was running, and I put my back out," he grimaced, "lot of pain. Is there somewhere I can lay flat 'till this eases up?"

"Like on the floor?" I asked.

"That would be perfect. Preferably not out here."

"There's a small hallway in back, it's where the trash bins are lined up."

"That sounds perfect. Lead the way."

I walked, he shuffled through the back room and into the adjacent hallway leading to the exit door. "It's just concrete," I said.

"That's fine." He grabbed my arm.

"Here, let me help you," I said giving him as much support at I could. "Should I call someone?"

"No. I just need to lie still for a few hours, 'till it eases up."

"Are you sure?"

"Yes. This is so embarrassing. Please don't tell anyone I'm back here."

"OK." He eased his way down to the ground and then onto his back, groaning the entire time. "Can I get you anything?"

"No... just a floor, quiet, and darkness."

"All right, if you need anything, please yell. Sure you don't need anything?"

"No." He straightened himself out and covered his face with his arms.

"Let me bring you some water at least." I went out front and returned with a cup of water, a few bottles of juice, a banana, and a hand full of straws.

"Bananas? When did we start selling bananas?"

"Only in the morning. We don't sell a lot, but it makes us look healthy." He laughed, then groaned. "I'm sorry. I'll leave you now. Call if you need anything." I pulled the door closed just as the phone rang.

I grabbed it as I passed the desk. "Thanks for calling the Inkwell."

"Hey..."

"Hi, Gregg, how are you?"

"Good, seen John yet?"

"John who?"

"John Banner, your CEO."

"Oh, the big guy." I glanced back at the closed door. "Why, is he in the area?"

"Office said he stayed just down the road from you."

"That's nice, we have a group of children coming in for storytime and hot chocolate, it will be a good day for him to visit."

"Give me a call when he gets there."

"I will."

Then it happened, the most blood curdling scream I had ever heard. "I gotta go!" I flung the back door open and burst into the café.

"What?"

"Gotta go Gregg, there's blood everywhere!"

I ran behind the counter and found Stephanie bent over with both hands covering her mouth and blood pouring out.

"I'm sorry, I'm so sorry. Are you OK? Oh God, I never saw you. I'm sorry, Stephanie are you ok?" Becca was on her knees pleading.

"Stephanie, are you all right? Here, you've got to sit down. Get me a chair," I called to Barry, who was sprinting around the corner. He grabbed the first one he passed and set it behind the counter. "Sit down, Steph." I helped her down into the chair as she kept both hands over her face. "Get me towels, lots of them. Becca, go fill a bag with ice."

"I'm sorry, I'm so sorry." Tears were flowing down Becca's cheeks.

"Becca, she needs ice, fill a towel from the bin," I instructed. Barry handed me a pile of clean white towels. I folded one and handed it to Stephanie who held it up to her mouth. "Ice, do you have the ice, Becca?"

"Yes, here it is." She handed me a towel so full of ice that I could hardly hold it. I opened it up and let half the cubes fall on the floor. I refolded and handed it to Stephanie. As she pulled the towel from her lips, I could see the gash that ran though her lips. She reached into her mouth and removed two large pieces of tooth.

"Oh, Steph." She looked up at me and placed the ice pack on her mouth. "Should I call your husband?" She nodded. "Do you know the number off-hand, or should I look it up?"

She held up her hand and began signing the digits. Barry picked up the phone and began dialing. He then handed it to me. "Thanks," I said. I had hoped he would make the call but no luck.

"Hey, this is Jenn at the café," I began.

"Hey, Jenn, how are things?"

"We had a little accident here, and Stephanie has a pretty big gash on her lips and has broken some teeth. Can you get over here?"

"What happened?" he asked.

"I'm not sure, I'll get it all figured out by the time you get here."

"Does she need an ambulance?"

"Steph, do you want an ambulance?" She shook her head. "She says no, I think the bleeding is stopping. Are you free to come?"

"I'll be right there."

Renee had just come on shift and as she walked towards the bar, I heard her surprised, "Oh, my God!"

"Can you and Barry handle the counter? We have twenty little kids coming in any minute, and we've got to get her in the back room."

"Sure," Renee said looking up at Barry. "But what happened?"

"It's all my fault. Stephanie, are you ok?"

"Becca, I'm going to take Stephanie in back. Can you get a bucket and get this mess cleaned up? Barry and Renee will take care of customers. You come back when it's all clean. And any towels with blood on them--let's put them in a separate bag, and we'll just toss them out." I helped Stephanie to her feet, and we walked into the back room.

"See if you can get Becca to tell you what happened," I said to Barry as we passed.

I led Stephanie to the desk and sat her down in the desk chair. I glanced over at the back door, it was still closed. I filled another towel with ice and handed it to her to replace the blood-saturated one in her hand. "Your husband will be here soon," I said. "Does it hurt?"

She nodded her head. "I'm sorry," I said.

I got another towel damp with warm water and began wiping the blood from her arms and neck. "What the hell happened?" I said quietly.

"The whipped cream container," Stephanie mumbled.

"The whipped cream container? You got hit with the container?"

She nodded. With her free hand she pointed toward the door. "Becca?" She nodded then began miming the shaking of the container and then pointed to her mouth. "Becca was making whipped cream and hit you with the container?" Stephanie nodded.

"Oh, my gosh, I am so sorry. That has to hurt like hell."

A few minutes later, Becca came through the door with a pile of red and white towels. Her eyes were red and swollen from crying. "Stephanie, OK? You OK? Oh, God, I'm so sorry," she kept repeating.

"Becca, tell me what happened."

"I was making the whipped cream. I was on the last canister. I had just put the charger on, and you know how we have to shake them? I was shaking it and turned around; I had no idea Stephanie was standing behind me."

"And you're the perfect height to nail her in the mouth."

"Yeah. Stephanie, don't hate me, I didn't mean to, really."

Stephanie reached out her hand and grabbed hold of Becca's. She did her best to smile through the tears and blood and towel. We sat quietly for the next few minutes, rubbing Stephanie's shoulders, replacing blood soaked towels with fresh clean ones. I kept glancing up at the closed door, hoping we weren't disturbing the other patient lying in pain behind them.

"Hi." We looked up to see a young, tall, and very distinguished man in scrubs walk through the back door. "How are you?" he said as he knelt down in front of Stephanie...she nodded.

I put my hand on his shoulder. "Steph got nailed by a metal whipped cream container... has to hurt."

"Let me see," he said, and she removed the ice. "Oh, Steph. It looks bad. You really got nailed. I think we need to go down to the ER. You may need some stitches." She shook her head. "We need to have Steve look at it; he's the best, I'll give him a call."

"Steph, you need to go get it looked at. Dr. Steve's the best, he tells us so every day. Let's get you a new towel. Becca, can you grab her bag and coat?"

"Let me toss these in the back by the trash," she said.

"NO!" I said abruptly. "Just put them down here, I'll double bag them."

A few minutes later, I accompanied Stephanie and her doctor husband slowly out the front door. They got in his car just as the school bus pulled into the parking lot.

"They're here!" I said. I ran around the counter to make sure all the blood and mess was cleaned up and to my surprise, Becca had done a pretty good job. "When they come in, direct them to the fireplace, we'll do story time first and drinks after. Is the storyteller here?"

"Just walked in, she's setting up," Barry said.

I went into the back room to retrieve Becca. "How are you doing?" I asked.

"OK - I think."

"I really need your help today, but I understand if you need to leave. That was pretty scary." She looked up at me and tears began to roll down her cheeks. I opened my arms, and she fell into them. I wrapped my arms around her, and that's where we stood when Gregg walked in the back door.

"Everything all right?" he asked.

I couldn't help but glance over to the closed door that hid the CEO from the rest of my world. "What are you doing here?" I asked.

"I was in the car when you hung up on me, thought I should swing by."

I released Becca. She dried her tears and wiped her hands on her apron. "You should take that apron off. Just put it on top of the pile of towels." She removed the apron and tossed it on the pile.

"Shit, what is that?" Gregg asked pointing to the pile of red and white towels.

I put my hand up to stop him. "I'll explain in a minute. Becca, think you can hold on 'till the kids are gone?"

"The kids!" she said. "I forgot about the kids."

"It would be great if you could get the hot cocoa made. I know Steph would appreciate it."

"Of course, it's the least I can do for her."

Becca put on a new apron and washed her hands, then returned to the café.

"Looks like a war zone," Gregg said.

"Close," I said.

"So what happened?"

"Becca – you know four-foot ten Becca, was shaking a whipped cream container, turned around, not knowing Stephanie was behind her, and she nailed her in the mouth. She's got a big gash, broken teeth. Her husband's a doctor and came to get her. They've gone to the hospital to see Dr. Steve, the plastic surgeon. What a mess."

"What can I do? Get these towels out back?" He bent over to pick them up.

"NO!" I shouted. He jumped back. "Leave them. Why is everyone so concerned about the trash? Any other day I would have had asked three times to get someone to take it out."

Gregg looked at me as if I had three heads, which on this day wouldn't have surprised me.

"Can you fill out the forms and make the calls we need to make for insurance? I've got twenty kids by the fireplace listening to *The Night Before Christmas* in need of hot cocoa."

At that moment, Suzie walked in for her shift.

"I've never been more relieved to see you!" I said.

"What's happening?" she exclaimed.

"Long story, I'll fill you in with all the bloody details. I need you out front, Renee and Barry have been running the counter for the last hour."

"On it," she said. "Want me to put those in the trash?"

"I'll take care of them," I said. "Just go take over the register, have Renee move to bar, and ask Barry to do a quick walk of the café."

She grabbed an apron and was gone. Gregg began to walk toward the desk; I grabbed his arm. "Can you call the insurance company from out there please?" I asked walking him toward the door.

I pulled him out into the café, where we found Becca filling the hot cocoa cups, Suzie greeting customers, Renee frothing milk, and Barry wiping off tables. It looked somewhat normal, like any other day. I looked around the corner and spotted twenty little people listening intently to their story. We walked a little closer, and I stood with Gregg as we listened.

I was lost in the story when I felt a warm hand on my shoulder. I turned my head. It was John Banner. "Thanks, Jenn... doing much better. The store looks great. I need to get back and check in. The office must think I've vanished. I'll be back later, and we can sit and chat. Thanks again for your help." He looked up at Gregg and nodded. He squeezed my shoulder again before letting go. Then the thin man in gray sweats, who had shuffled into my store a few hours earlier, slowly walked to the front door and made his exit.

"Was that...?" Gregg began. I smiled and nodded. I hooked my arm around Gregg's and drew my attention back to the little people. "Where did he come from? How long has he been here?"

"Doesn't really matter. He's coming back, you can ask him later. Did your mom read this to you when you were a kid?" I asked glancing up at him. He was focused on the front door. I began reciting, "He spoke not a word, but went straight to his work, and filled all the stockings, then turned with a jerk. And laying his finger aside of his nose, and giving a nod, up the chimney he rose. He sprang, (well shuffled,) to his sleigh, to his team gave a whistle, and away they all flew like the down of a thistle. [*What is the down of a thistle?*] But I heard him exclaim, 'ere he drove out of sight, 'Happy Christmas to all and to all *a good night.*'" I unhooked my arm and patted Gregg on the shoulder. "Merry Christmas, Gregg, I've got bloody towels to get rid of, and you have a few calls to make. I'll pull Stephanie's file for you."

As I walked toward the back room, I glanced back at him. Gregg was still standing there looking in the direction the man in gray had gone.

"Hey," I called out. He turned back toward me, "You look like you've seen the Ghost of Christmas Past. It's Christmas Gregg, and you have calls to make." I disappeared into the back room.

Bringing in the

New Year!

Join us New Years Eve as we

Ring in the New Year.

Live music all night!

Inkwell Cafe

22 | The Eve of a New Year

The week after Christmas I received two notices. The first informed me that Stephanie would not be returning as the accident had caused a great deal of dental work. We found out after the incident that Stephanie had spent thousands of dollars on her smile at the beginning of her modeling career, and the hit to the mouth from the whipped cream canister had almost obliterated it. It was all just too much for her to deal with, and she needed time.

The second came as no surprise; Jackie was dropping out of the master's program, and moving north to live for a year in a friend's cabin. She would work 'till the end of the year. I wasn't sure this was a good life choice for her. My imagination went a little haywire when I thought of life in a cabin in the woods for a year--where would she find a refrigerator to take out her anger on?

The last five weeks had been a blur, but the holidays are like that. Just a few more days and we would be welcoming the new year and new beginnings. I walked out on the patio and headed to our corner table where the Roaster, the Baker, and Suzie were waiting.

"We have to replace Steph," I said with a frown. "She isn't coming back."

"That's too bad," Barry said. "We'll miss her."

"Got any ideas for replacements?"

"Suzie, why don't you give it a try?" Renee asked.

"I don't think so. Too many strange people."

"Strange!" I said. "Who isn't?"

"What about Ruth Ann?" Suzie offered.

"Who's Ruth Ann again?" I asked.

"She comes for the painting classes. Short, retired, she wears the big brimmed hat with a sunflower sticking out of it."

"The Sunflower Fairy? Do you think she would be interested?"

"She seems really social, and I think she knows everyone in town. People are always greeting her."

"Interesting. Anyone know how to get a hold of her?"

"The painters meet tomorrow morning. If she's not there, maybe someone could contact her."

"I'll scout her out tomorrow."

"I hear Jackie's leaving?"

"This is her last week. I don't think we need to replace her just yet; let's see what business is like in January."

"Hard to believe we're still in our first year," Renee said.

"Seems like a lifetime already," Barry added.

"We're just tired, really tired," I said. "All right folks, open those calendars, what do we have going for New Year's Eve?"

"Food is all set, we're trying sandwiches," Barry said.

"Sandwiches! Really? Go figure. I love that idea! I've always thought we could do a decent light lunch/dinner serving. Gregg know about this?" I asked.

"We're meeting this week, I'll roll it out then."

"Looks to me like Steph has all the entertainment lined up. A really nice collection, should be a mellow night. Oh, and I met our bouncer."

"Bouncer?" Suzie squealed. "Are you kidding? We don't need a bouncer."

"Officer Rick recommended him. Nice guy."

New Year's Eve arrived. We had promoted the Inkwell as an alternative hangout for the night. We weren't the place you go after you've had too much to drink. Those were the people our bouncer would prevent from entering. I don't want any puking in my store.

Daniel arrived around 11:00 p.m., and we took a table on the patio. A cello player was sitting on the makeshift stage between the fireplace and bakery. It was a clear night and the orange/red glow of the heaters lit up the patio.

"It's a gorgeous night," I said.

"Doesn't get much better than this," Daniel said. From the patio we could see the bonfires that lined the beach. "Why don't we do this more often?"

"Because we don't serve beer or tequila," I said.

"We could sneak it in," he suggested.

"Someone just got fired for that."

"What, whiskey in their coffee?"

"No, vodka in their orange juice."

"Seriously?"

"Yep. Couldn't make this shit up. He would nurse his ex-large orange juice all morning. Come to find out, it was mixed with vodka."

"How did they find out?"

"I don't know, I'm guessing because he suddenly was friendly."

Daniel just shook his head, "It is a strange little world you live in, isn't it?"

"It really is. It's no wonder there are stories of complete villages going to ruin once coffee was introduced. Guess everyone enjoys coffee breaks. It's an interesting commodity, The Devil's Brew, or so it's been called."

We sat quietly listening to the guitar. "Here she is," I heard Becca say from behind me. "It's Gregg," she said handing me the phone.

"Happy New Year," I said.

"How's it going?"

"Good, I think. Nice steady flow of customers. Haven't had any issues yet."

"Tell him I like the whiskey addition but would also like to see scotch," Daniel whispered.

"Daniel says he likes the whiskey addition, but would really like us to serve scotch."

Gregg laughed and then was quiet. "You're not really serving whiskey, are you?"

"What do you think?"

"I'm not surprised by anything anymore."

"If I were serving alcohol, it would be tequila, and I would be pocketing the money. You're meeting with Barry this week, correct?"

"I think so."

"He's got some great ideas, the menu he came up with for tonight is excellent. He's a good guy. It may be the late hour talking, or the stars, or night air. I don't know. I may even deny this in the morning, but thanks for this store, Gregg. I'm loving it."

"I don't hear that too often," he said. "I'm glad you're enjoying it."

"We won't speak of it again--ever." Out of the corner of my eye, I saw a woman walk in. "Oh, God no, please no!"

"What?" I heard in stereo from the man sitting next to me and the one on the phone.

"She's here."

"Who?" Again in unison.

"The recorder chick. Steph said she's getting better but I don't want to find out," I scooted myself to the end of the chair preparing for my getaway.

"Why would she schedule her tonight?" Daniel asked.

"I don't know, but it doesn't matter. I think this is our cue to leave."

"Tell Daniel Happy New Year. You two get out of there and go home," Gregg suggested.

"Sorry, Gregg, I forgot you were there. Thanks, you too. Now go find your real wife and celebrate the New Year."

Daniel reached out, grabbed my arm, and pulled me back into my seat. "Let's finish this last song," he said.

We welcomed the New Year in on the patio of the Inkwell Café under the stars and warmth of the heaters and the cello playing, *What Are You Doing New Year's Eve?*

Inkwell Art Show

Friday - Sunday

Painting, Scuptures, Glass,
Photos
&
Live Music!

Inkwell Cafe

23 | A New Year

January arrived, and the slowing down of business that I had anticipated never happened. By now, we had a plethora of regular customers; for many, we were their extended family. We likely knew more about them and their lives than their relatives did.

Before leaving, Stephanie had arranged an art show which was scheduled to start on Friday afternoon and end Sunday evening. All the artists were signed up and a waiting list created for the overflow. I had met Ruth Ann, and she agreed to assist us with the show. It was a way for her to see what was expected and for us to see just how connected she was.

Ruth Ann retired a few years after she lost her husband. She was one of those women who lived with so much energy, she bounced when she walked. Her children were grown, and she raved about her grandkids. She and I hit it off immediately, and I hoped that the art show would prove to both of us that she was a perfect fit for the position.

As promised, Suzie began reminding our customers that her birthday was the following month. She did a daily countdown when it was exactly one month away. "You have twenty-nine days to shop," we heard her say. "It's just twenty days to pick out my perfect gift," she said as she handed them their receipt. "Ten more days, write it down."

"Do you want your birthday off?" I asked, as I filled in the schedule for February.

"No!" she shot back at me. "Who will receive my gifts?"

"Are you getting gifts?" I asked.

"I sure better be," she said. "You got your shopping done?"

"Sure, I'm buying you a pound of coffee."

"Perfect," she said, "just what I always wanted."

"Seriously, do you want your birthday off?"

"Seriously--NO!" she said.

"All right, no bitching that morning when you're working on your birthday, which is apparently the most holy day of the year. Oh, look who I'm saying that to." I went back to my work. "And by the way, I asked the recorder lady to be here first thing to play Happy Birthday for you."

"What a lovely thought," she said. "I heard she's improved."

At noon on Friday, the artists began arriving with cases, trunks, and vans filled with their masterpieces. We lined the walls, set up display tables, and floated prints in the windows. The café was a buzz of creative energy. We had pictures of sunsets, still life paintings, a table of glass vases that were blown locally. Ruth Ann was charming and organized, and Renee was right, she knew everyone.

"Jenn," she said as she came into the back room, "I think you should see this."

"What?" I asked hoping she would give me insight before leading me out into the café blind.

"There's an artist out there with nudes," she wrinkled her forehead.

"Really?" She nodded. "Is it tasteful?"

"Sure, but they're nudes," she said.

"I wonder if Steph knew."

"I checked the list and it looks like it."

The back door swung open, "Hey, boss, there's a bunch of naked ladies lined up next to the bakery. Not that I mind, but I'm thinking some parents might."

"I just heard," I said. "Got any suggestions?"

"What about a screen?" Ruth Ann said.

"Perfect. Do we have one?"

"I've not seen one," Barry said.

"Got your car today?"

"Yes," he said.

"Can you run down the street? They should have one in that furniture store."

Barry took off his apron and set out on the mission to find a screen. Ruth Ann and I walked out into the café. "Introduce me to the artist," I said.

We walked back toward the bakery and Ruth Ann introduced me to the twenty-something artist.

I walked down the line of his artwork. "It's beautiful," I said. "You are really talented." He smiled. *And now I have to tell you that I have to hide your work.* I studied the paintings a few moments longer. "I'm sorry I have to do this, but I think we are going to have to protect your work a little."

He tilted his head, "Protect MY work?"

"Actually, protect the kids that come in here. To be very honest, protect ourselves from the parents of the kids that come in here."

He began to laugh. "No one has ever been that honest. What do we need to do?"

"Barry is running out to purchase a screen. We'll display it on the back of the screen so they have to walk around to see it. If we keep it set up back here, whoever is working the bakery can keep an eye out and ensure it doesn't become the hang-out for our younger audience. Are you all right with that?" He nodded.

"Good. Thanks for being so understanding."

Barry returned with a screen, and we somehow maneuvered it to hold the entire collection. The screen sat in front of the bakery counter all weekend. Ten naked women watching Barry and his team bake delicacies for three days.

On Saturday afternoon, I found myself behind the register as an older woman walked through the door. She stopped and looked around. The café was alive with people--regular customers filling the seats and art afficionados surveying the exhibit. She walked over to the counter. "A small coffee," she said.

I rang her up and poured her coffee. As I handed it to her, I saw her hand shaking. "Is there a place close by where we can eat?" she asked.

"Are you visiting?"

"Sort of," she said. "We have someone in the hospital." She took a tissue from her pocket and wiped her nose. Tears began to escape through the corners of her eyes.

"I'm so sorry," I said. "Is there anything else I can get you?"

She shook her head and forced a smile, and then the world stopped. For the next several moments she shared her story with me. Her daughter-in-law had tried for years to have a baby, and four months ago they found out they were expecting triplets. She told me how excited they all were when it happened. She told me of the phone call two days ago telling them that there were issues, and the call yesterday morning informing them that she was on the way to the hospital because there was something terribly wrong. They took the first flight they could book and arrived without sleep, food, or even knowing what she had packed. I listened and the world stood still.

There were hordes of people in my café, live music being played in the back corner; there were six employees on the clock, but for those few moments, no one was within twenty feet of us. No one interrupted our conversation, nothing came between this sweet lady, who needed to tell someone of her heartache, and myself, the receiver. The world had stopped, and I was fortunate enough to observe it happening.

She wiped her nose and dabbed the tears from her eyes. "She's lost all three," she said.

I reached across the counter and held her hand. "I'm so very sorry," I said as I squeezed it. "There are things that happen in our lives that there are no answers for, no reason, no explanation. Do you know where you are staying?" She nodded. "All you can do is to be there for them." My eyes began to well up, and the world remained quiet. "If you need anything while you are here, give us a call." I took a business card from the counter and wrote my name on the back. "It doesn't seem like it right now, but it will be all right." She squeezed my hand and then wiped the tears, and the world remained silent.

I've had a handful of such experiences. Smack dab in the middle of a normal day when someone I've never met, and will never meet again, needs for me to listen to them. It's an out-of-body experience as if my peripheral vision recognizes that in an instant, the world around me has become still and quiet, allowing me to listen intently to the one who needs to be heard.

She picked up her coffee and walked out the front doors, and the life around me once again began to beat. "Someone you know?" Becca asked, making her way to the register.

"No, complete stranger," I said watching her vanish into the night.

"She OK?"

"Probably not. We may see her again. If you do, give her whatever she asks."

"You OK?"

"I will be."

I watched the front door all weekend waiting for her to walk back through the doors. She never did. She was there for a moment. And I was grateful to be the one at the register.

Caffeine Contents

8 oz. Cup = 85 to 110 milligrams.

Espresso-single shot = 35 to 45 milligrams.

Brewed tea weighs in at about 40 milligrams.

Chocolate = from 10 to 20 milligrams. (Milk chocolate is less than dark.)

An entire coffee tree of average size = approximately 6000 milligrams.

A 150 lb. bag of coffee = approximately 510,000 milligrams.

24 | February

Suzie's birthday finally arrived. We had heard her count it down for the past 29 days. "Hey, boss," Barry said, as he ducked into the back room. "I'm a little concerned that Suzie has this whole birthday thing blown out of proportion. She could be really disappointed."

"You think?" I responded.

He nodded. "Yeah. If no one shows up with gifts, she may have a meltdown."

"What should we do?" I was actually touched by his concern. If it weren't for the age difference, I had always wondered if those two would make it as a couple.

"I'll make a cake this afternoon after she leaves. At least we can have that for her," he said shrugging his shoulders.

"That's really thoughtful," I said. "I'm in at nine tomorrow, I'll pick up some flowers--maybe some balloons."

The next morning, I arrived at the front door with a small bouquet of wildflowers. As I opened the door, I realized I was the back-up date, and the real date had arrived with two dozen long-stem roses. The front counter was lined with vases of flowers, a table had been pulled over and sat next to the register to hold all the gift bags and packages. Balloons were tied to anything that would hold them down, filling the ceiling with balls of color. And standing behind the register was Suzie, wearing a tiara.

"Excuse me," I heard from behind. I was so taken aback by the display that I didn't realize I was standing in the middle of the door.

"Oh, I'm sorry," I said and moved out of the way. I had never seen anything like it. In nearly twenty years, I had never had an employee pull something like this off. I watched as another dozen balloons floated through the front door.

"Are these for me?" the tiara wearing crazy lady behind the counter said. The customer nodded. "However did you know it was my birthday?" she said as sweetly and innocently as any southern belle could.

I walked into the back room with Barry was right behind me. "So," I said flinging my pathetic collection of wildflowers at him, "you think she's going to be disappointed?"

He laughed. "She's got more loot out there than she'll know what to do with."

"Did you bake that cake?" I asked.

"I did. She actually saw it this morning and made me bend over so she could give me a kiss. She acted like it was the greatest gift in the world."

"She's one of a kind," I said shaking my head.

"Wait, it gets better," he said. "Triple shot over ice and cranberry scone is sending lunch over for all of us."

"You're kidding."

"No. Did you know he owns the pub down on the beach? The one right next to the pier."

"I had no idea. That's his? That's quite the operation."

"I know. I wonder if he's hiring?"

"Don't even think about it," I said in my most motherly tone. "We need you right here. Besides, where else would you find a tiara sporting chick who asks you to bend over so she can thank you with a kiss?"

"Good point," he said.

As the day continued, so did the steady flow of gifts. Suzie wasn't fazed by any of it... just another day at the Inkwell. If she had it her way, every day would be her birthday.

Suzie's birthday started the week out with a bang, but all the air was quickly let out of our sails as one by one, the entire team came down with the flu. By Friday morning, we were down to three, Suzie, Barry, and myself. At 6:00 a.m., I saw Barry dash down the hall leading to the restrooms and my heart stopped. Five minutes later, he was putting his coat on and waving goodbye as he walked out the front doors.

Suzie and I just looked at each other. "What are we going to do?" I asked.

"Serve coffee, I guess," she said.

"Do you want to be on the bar?" I asked.

"Hell, no!" she said.

I scanned the café, it was clean. "It will last about two hours before we have to get out there." I opened each of the refrigerators taking mental note of the inventory of milk and other supplies. "I think we can make it 'till nine," I said forcing myself to exhale. "It's like watching a sinking ship and trying to figure out how much time you have left before you have to learn to swim." We both laughed and took our positions. Suzie was armed and ready at the register and I at the bar.

"When does the next one come in?" she asked.

"Becca's here at 1:00 p.m."

"You closing?" Suzie asked.

"I think I'm here all day," I said trying not to think about it. I found myself glancing up at the clock, hoping the day was flying past us. Unfortunately, each time I looked up, five minutes had passed.

"Ex-large Latte," I called out.

"Quiet in here today," the recipient said. I glanced at the door and counted eight people in line. "Where's your team?"

"Oh, you mean *that quiet*. Unfortunately, they've all shared a bug; the whole group is down for the count. Suzie and I are the last two remaining. Want a job? We can get you up and running in minutes."

"No, thanks," he said. "Hope your day goes quickly," and he toasted me with his drink.

"Thanks," I said, as I poured the milk into two more drinks.

Ten of those five minute glances had passed when a familiar face entered. He wasn't good on the bar and had no idea how to enter an order on the register, but he could wash dishes and wipe down tables. "Why are you here?" I asked.

"Thought you might need some help. Barry here?" I shook my head. "Not him, too?" I nodded and called three more drinks.

"What can I do?" Gregg asked.

"Really?"

"Yes, I'll be happy to go if I'm not needed..."

"Listen," I heard Suzie order, "if you're going to work with me, you better be on time--which means early--with hands washed and apron on. I need coffee brewed. You think you can handle that?" Gregg nodded and in less than a minute was standing in front of the brewers making a fresh batch of coffee.

"You're not in uniform," she continued. "Next time be prepared." He nodded. "You don't like our uniform?" He looked back at me for reassurance that she was kidding. "Be careful. You could find yourself in brown polyester saying, 'do you want fries with that?'" Suzie looked up at him through her eyebrows. Three seconds later Gregg lost his always professional composure and was bent over the counter, holding his side, howling. I simply shook my head and called the next drink.

We sped along for the next hour. When customers inquired about the new face behind the counter and the lack of familiar faces, Suzie told them that aliens had landed on the roof and sucked everyone out, that she and I had hid in the walk-in refrigerator in the back room, that the aliens had left this one--she jerked her head back in Gregg's direction--as a replacement, and we are in negotiations because we don't like 'this one' and want our other ones back.

By the third time she said it, we had our parts memorized. When she referred to 'this one', Gregg would wave or bow his head. When she told of the hiding in the fridge, I would motion that it was just the two of us. And when she got to the negotiations, I would nod in agreement, all the while calling drinks, keeping an eye on the milk supply, scanning the café, and of course, glancing up every five minutes in hopes the day was over.

At five minutes before eight there was a slight lull. "Get the café," Suzie instructed and Gregg dutifully grabbed a towel. "Take some creamers with you, just switch them out, we'll fill them later." Arms filled with cold creamers and towel in his hand, Gregg headed out into the café. Suzie began brewing more coffee and counted to make sure there was enough coffee measured out to get us through the next hour. I darted into the back room and filled a cart with gallons of milk. As I filled the refrigerators, I glanced up at the clock. 8:00 a.m. had finally arrived--it would be our busiest hour of the day.

On a typical Friday, we would serve four hundred customers by 10:00 a.m. There would be seven people working in order to make this happen. Today, there were two and a half of us.

The Invisible Man arrived on cue, and Suzie had his drink ready for him. I watched as he took his normal place in the café and then I forgot about him. At 8:30 a.m., I checked the time report on the bar screen, forty-six customers in the last half hour. "I still got it," I said out loud.

"What?" Suzie yelled back.

"Forty-six bar drinks in the last half hour. That's more than one a minute. Do you want to switch now?"

"You're funny," she said. "Did you ever consider being a comedian?" I don't think she even took a breath before she began her alien story for the zillionth time that morning. Gregg waved and nodded, and I did my bit on cue and called four more drinks.

"How's bakery?" I asked during the next lull.

"Doesn't matter," Suzie replied, "Nothing we can do about it."

"You're right! Never mind," I said. "You know how to bake?" I asked Gregg, expecting for him to deny any such skill.

"I do!" he said. We both gasped.

"You do?" Suzie asked in a tone that was less than confident. "Can you get the afternoon stuff out?" He nodded. "You mean you're not just *Corporate Candy*?" We all burst into laughter.

"Don't make me laugh," I said. "I have to *constipate!*"

"You what?" Gregg spit out, his face all crinkled up.

"She has issues, you know, you've worked with her long enough. But we *are* an equal opportunity employer," Suzie said. She handed the next customer his coffee and change then she dropped her hands to her side, leaned her head back and looked up at the ceiling. "Bring them back," she said. "Bring them back! You can take him instead!" She reached over and grabbed Gregg's arm, attempting to lift him toward the alien mothership.

"Stop it. If I break my stride, I'll never get it back!" I ordered in-between bursts of laughter, gasps for air, and calling out mochas, lattes, and whatever. "Tomorrow we're going to have Serve Yourself Saturday. If you want it, get back here and make it! Large Vanilla Latte," I called out in my nice voice. A woman reached out and took the drink. "Thank you ma'am. Have a great day."

"You, too," she said.

"Too late," I said, "but there's always tomorrow."

I glanced up at the clock, two more five-minute glances had passed, it was 8:45 a.m. "It's never going to end. This day is never going to end...small decaf, cappuccino."

I glanced back at the computer screen and was reaching for the next required cup, when I heard the all too familiar sound of water being squeezed out of a towel. Out of the corner of my eye, I saw both Suzie and Gregg at the registers. I jerked around. Behind me a man of average height, average looks, who wore a light brown coat, was bent over the bucket of sanitized water used for cleaning off tables. He stood up, smiled, winked, and headed toward the condiment counter and began straightening the creamers and wiping the surface.

"Suzie," I said much louder than intended. She spun around. I pointed. She saw him immediately. We both stood there watching as he moved out into the café, wiping off tables and collecting cups and plates that had been left behind. With his arms full, he walked back toward the bar. I watched as he pushed the back door open and walked through as if he had done it a hundred times before. He emerged seconds later with empty arms and headed out to collect more. After one more round, he placed his towel back into the bucket of water, took a paper towel from the dispenser, and dried his hands. He looked up at me, smiled, nodded, and took his leave.

"What the..." Suzie began.

"No idea..." I finished.

"Did I miss something?" Gregg interrupted.

"The invisible man--just appeared," I said. "Large Mocha," I called out.

"Hey, it's my first husband," Suzie hollered. I glanced over to see my husband walking past the register. Daniel laughed. "I'm his second wife," she told the next customer, "I just have to figure out how to get rid of her!" Suzie said pointing in my direction.

Daniel threw her a kiss and made his way around the counter. He stood next to the bar and greeted Gregg with the nod that men use to say *hello*.

"What are you doing here?"

"Took a sick day," he said.

"You're not sick, are you?" I asked, fearful of the answer.

"No, but I heard you all are," he said.

"Ain't that the truth," a customer said, waiting for his drink.

"Hey, be nice or I'll give you decaf instead of regular today," I replied.

"Thought you might need some help," Daniel said.

"You did? That's wonderful. I don't know how we're going to make it to the end."

"I can't do much, but I can clear tables and wash dishes," he said.

"In this company, that qualifies you for a regional position," Suzie said, elbowing Gregg as he handed a blueberry muffin to the next guest.

"Know what happened a year ago?" Daniel asked.

"Couldn't tell you what happened an hour ago," I said.

"I was glancing back through last year's calendar and saw a note on this day, *Jenn's second interview*."

"No!" I said trying to recall. "Large decaf Americano--thanks, have a great day. A year?"

"I guess it was," Gregg said. "How did a year fly by so quickly? You're getting old," he said looking directly at me.

"Thanks," I said, "I can't believe it, really?"

Daniel was right, it was a year ago. It had been an eventful year, it had been an exhausting year, it had been a really great year. As the four of us worked together for the next several hours, we reminisced about all that had happened: our Grand Opening, Kenneth allegedly taking the trash out, 10 Alarm Lattes, the woman who peed in the dark.

At 1:00 p.m., Becca received the warmest welcome ever offered at the Inkwell, and I gladly relinquished my position at the bar. At 2:00 p.m., Barry phoned informing us he did not have the flu, he thought it was bad fish from the night before and would be able to come back around 5:00 p.m. to close. Gregg baked way too much product, and we decided to offer brownies and pie for Saturday breakfast. Daniel washed dishes and cleaned the refrigerators before he attempted putting the milk order away.

Suzie stayed at the register, welcoming guests, brewing coffee, repeating her alien story, and did what she was best at--being fabulous.

...and I did everything else!

The White Cover

For anyone who has used a cafe for an office, we not only share our love for coffee but also the coffee stains that we carry with us. They are on our calendars, reports, resumes, schedules, and any other type of work that we may have compiled while enjoying our favorite latte.

The cover of this book is a clean slate that will also earn its own coffee stains. When it does, please do me a favor. Post a picture of your read, loved and stained cover to my Instagram or Facebook pages: @jeanniebruenning

For additional coffee facts, check out these sites:

www.espressocoffeeguide.com

www.dilworthcoffee.com

www.specialty-coffee-advisor.com

A Note from the Author

Life in a cafe is never dull. The stories in this book are real; I can recall each one as they actually happened. Luckily, they didn't all happen in one year but over the course of a career.

Cafes are a special place. They are comfort, community and conversation. They bring strangers together and make them family. There is nothing else quite like it.

Jeannie Bruenning

Author ~ Publisher ~ Teacher

After working in the corporate business world for over three decades, Jeannie started a boutique publishing company on the coast of California in a small beach town. Being an author herself, she is passionate about the writer's journey. You can find her most days at her family's hacienda in the beautiful hills of the Central Coast or in her Jeep Wrangler, parked on the warm sands of Pismo Beach, California.

Connect with Jeanniewww.jeanniebruenning.com

www.ingramcontent.com/pod-product-compliance
Lightning Source LLC
Chambersburg PA
CBHW022157260626
47155CB00019B/3058